THE ENDURANTS

Published by WordCrafts Press
Cody, Wyoming 82414
www.wordcrafts.net

THE
ENDURANTS

a novel

KL Palmer

WordCrafts Press

1

Leo was late. It was the first day of the last class of spring
semester—his last semester of college. His attention however, was quickly fading. He would be the first to admit
he'd rather be riding his mountain bike along the winding
rivers outside the city. He didn't know what he'd do after
graduation, but he knew he didn't want to be in any class
for one more day.

When he walked into the classroom, all eyes turned toward
him. The young professor casually leaned against the bank
of windows on the opposite side of the room, but unlike
most teachers who would be distracted and draw attention
to the interruption or make the person at fault feel inferior,
he ignored Leo and continued his review of the syllabus he'd
just made note of.

Leo took the last remaining seat that formed a circle
around the small room. He smiled crookedly at a pretty girl
who shyly watched him from across his table.

∼

Fiona dropped her eyes as soon as Leo looked at her. She
was caught staring and became uncomfortable when he made
it known with his nice smile. And it was nice. He was a good

looking guy. The small class had a few nice looking guys. She blushed just thinking about them.

Why was she so nervous? She wasn't cheating on Matt. He was working at the hospital in Manhattan through his internship. They'd been apart since she started at the university in upstate New York. She'd be with him when she finished a year from now, and they'd get married after he took a full time position in the cardiology department. It would be the fairy tale ending she'd been waiting for.

I bet she came here on daddy's money, Ro thought. She had watched Fiona enter the room. *She walks like she has more than anyone. And her clothes are definitely designer. I can't handle much more of this.*

Ro—actually Rowena—was anything but rich. Her mom and dad hocked family heirlooms to keep her in the beauty pageants she competed in while growing up. It was a first place scholarship that got her through her first two years of college. Now she worked as a bartender to stay there. She was determined to make it through until the end and become the first person in her family to get a college degree. Then as a journalist, she'd become famous with a nationwide breaking news story and get her parents out of the trailer park they lived in. At least that was the dream she hoped to pursue one day.

Zane gave Ro a once over. His eyes stopped a minute on her chest. Her shirt was low cut, and he couldn't help but look. His girlfriend Veronica sat to his left. She saw him stare and cut her eyes at him while squeezing hard on his thigh under the table. He let out a quick yelp while shifting in his seat. Veronica smiled across the table to anyone who might have heard Zane. In the three years they'd been together she had come to realize he would always be a flirt. She still loved him, though.

Yes, that girl is very pretty, she admitted to herself. *She looks like Snow White with her fair skin, jet black hair, and red lipstick. But Snow White never showed that much cleavage.*

Her hand didn't stray too far from Zane's leg—for the next time she needed to reign his attention back in.

Piper saw what Veronica did and smiled back to show she agreed with her reaction. She couldn't help giggle when Zane let out the cry of pain.

I'm gonna like this girl, she thought. *We could easily be friends. She has the guts to do what I always wanted to do to my ex when he did the same thing. Maybe if I had, he wouldn't have started talking with Bianca, the last one he looked at, and then quickly slept with.*

Just thinking about it turned her stomach, and she sighed deeply, biting her lip before focusing back on the professor as he spoke.

This was Joey Harrison's second year teaching at the school. He got his master's and doctorate degrees one after the other and right before his firstborn came along. He had married his high school girlfriend before they even went to college, but they were disciplined in focusing on school, getting degrees, and starting careers before a family. They almost made it. Joey was over half way done with his doctorate program when Layla became pregnant. He walked the stage to accept his degree the same day Layla found out they were having a son. He began his teaching career at the community college they lived near but accepted this full time position at the state university only eighteen months later. He had to commute almost an hour each way, but the extra income was worth it. Now, as he approached thirty, he was the proud father of not one but two sons.

Ezra was named after his Israeli great-grandfather. He grew up being teased about it almost daily. And that was even in the Christian school he was forced to attend. But as he looked from the syllabus to Mr. Harrison he wondered why a grown man would still go by the name of *Joey* and not *Joe* or *Joseph*. He assumed that was what Joey was short for. He'd have to remember to ask him that. He also wondered how old his professor really was. He had to be young, maybe late 20s—30 at most—but he looked really young regardless.

Must be the Clark Kent glasses he wears, Ezra thought.

He wondered why anyone still wore that style of glasses. And that t-shirt and relaxed jeans with flip flops. Mr. Harrison wasn't like any instructor he'd ever seen. Ezra began to doodle as his mind tried to answer his silent questions.

During introductions, did he say his name was Ezra? That is so cool. And to think 'Indya' won't be the only odd name in the room.

It wasn't that Indya didn't like her name—she actually

loved it. She was an urban socialite, and the fact that she could stand out in any way made her truly happy. She kept her mocha skin shimmering with glitter powder, her short dark hair spiked in style, and her wardrobe updated with the seasonal fashion changes. She quickly became mesmerized in watching Ezra's quick strokes of his sketches around the edge of his copy of the syllabus.

He'll have competition in the doodling department though, she thought. Fashion design was her specialty. She was going to work in Paris one day. Her designs would headline the runway. She smiled thinking about it.

Ken was known as *Keno* to most people. He'd been Keno since playing football in junior high school. As odd as it was to have one Ken, there were two in his grade—Ken Ballard and him, Ken Olson. To distinguish between to the two they added their last initial to the roster and were referred to Ken B and Ken O for the remainder of their sports days. By the time he got to high school Ken O turned into Keno, and he now was hardly ever called Ken, and would probably never answer to it. One his college application he put *Keno* in the nickname slot and had been Keno ever since.

He couldn't help but watch the stylish petite classmate two seats away as Indya tapped her high stilettoed foot under the table. *What a tall shoe*, he pondered. *She might be a force to be reckoned with. That fire might be too hot for me to even get near.*

Ty remembered playing Keno in football. He broke his leg during the season opener of their senior year, and it was

Keno's team he was playing against that day. Although it was only a little more than a year ago he didn't think Keno would remember.

He still had a slight limp, and the old injury acted up whenever the weather started to turn wet. He remembered laughing at his grandma when she complained about her joints aching when the weather changed. Now he understood what she meant. He stretched his leg out into the middle of the circle and rotated his foot to try to alleviate the increasing pain.

It is going to rain this evening, he thought. His leg was a better predictor of the weather than any meteorologist on television.

Arch got his knee brushed by the stretch of Ty's leg under the table. Ty didn't realize it, and Arch pulled his leg back to get out of his way. It didn't bother him. He didn't want to draw attention to the invasion of his personal space, and instead leaned closer to the table and propped his arm in front of him.

He had already read the paper Mr. Harrison gave out at the beginning of class. He was, as usual, the first one to show up and had plenty of time to get settled.

This should be interesting, he thought with more than a bit of exasperation.

His academic advisor had miscalculated what was required at the beginning of the semester, but the man didn't seem the least bit apologetic when he informed Arch that he still needed one more elective to graduate. There were very few classes that weren't full and that worked for his schedule. So here he was—even though he had no idea what this class was about or even how to pronounce the name of the course.

2

The class was Eschatology. It was a 10-week theology course offered to fulfill an elective requirement at the university. *Eschatology: the study of the final events of history and the ultimate destiny of the human race.* Mr. Harrison described the class as an open discussion course that would involve a lot of roundtable debating, team-driven assignments, and no tests or quizzes. Quiet shouts of approval waved across the circle, but Mr. Harrison was quick to continue his requirements.

"There will, however be a lot of work that is done in this room, and participation is necessary—every day. You can't just come in when you want or just plan to sit here and listen. Without tests to accumulate points it's hard to catch up when you aren't here. Make sense?"

A few nods confirmed what was heard. A guilty look fell on Leo's face, and he pursed his lips to keep from smiling. Indya's hand shot up before Mr. Harrison could continue.

He nodded at her to go ahead, and she asked, "So are we studying like the Bible and Revelations and earth-destroying asteroids?"

The classes erupted in laughter, and Mr. Harrison smiled before answering. "Yes, we will. We'll talk about all that. We will discuss things you've never heard of, things you don't want to hear, and stuff you will most definitely want to know. You will remember this class for a long time, and best part— you'll remember your classmates. I can't tell you how many classes I've taken in my life where I didn't know anyone but the teacher's name, and even that is foggy. That won't happen here. I promise."

Ty and Fiona looked up at each other and then caught the eyes of the other students as everyone glanced around.

"We're about to get out of here for today, but before coming back next time I want you all to bring lists and questions: lists of what you think we will talk about it class, questions on what you don't understand about Eschatology, and what you'd like to know more about. Our first assignment will be comparing these lists. So get creative. Until then, it was great meeting all of you and happy research."

He turned and walked toward his desk in the corner of the room. It had been pushed against the wall, and the only thing on it was a backpack and tall thermos of coffee. As Mr. Harrison zipped the bag and grabbed the mug, the class quietly disbursed. Veronica and Zane automatically held hands and turned right down the hall. Some people followed them; the rest turned left. Nobody spoke to each other.

3

Piper tightened her short blonde ponytail and shifted to get more comfortable in her chair. Slowly the circle filled in, and every chair became occupied. She watched Veronica and Zane caress each other's hands as they whispered and giggled together. He stared into her brown eyes, and she subtly flirted by flipping her long brunette hair over her shoulder and tilting her head. Piper smiled at their affection.

Beside her, Fiona rolled her eyes at the same display.

Mr. Harrison dropped his backpack on the desk in the same spot as last time. He moved to the windows and crossed his arms. After a quick welcome back, he asked who wanted to start with their list.

"Ideas or questions first?" Keno asked.

"However you want to do it," Mr. Harrison responded.

Beginning with Keno, and with each person following, thoughts on what Eschatology was and questions on what the class would be about began to flow. Some people referenced the Bible—specifically books of Daniel and Revelation—and the meteors that Indya talked about. Others listed a multitude of natural disasters, global warming, and nuclear destruction from another world war.

Some students wondered when the world would end—if

there would be warnings before it happened, how many generations the earth had left, and what secrets are being kept from the public.

"That's an interesting one," Mr. Harrison noted. "This is the first time that question has come up in all the times that I have taught this course." He stopped for a few moments, as if thinking of what to say before answering. "Yes, I think we will most definitely talk about that."

"What do *you* believe will happen?" Ro asked, as she twirled a strand of her hair.

Mr. Harrison walked toward the front of the room, and everyone shifted in their seats to watch him. "I think as class goes on you will get a better understanding of what I believe, what I think will happen, and is happening. But that doesn't mean I expect any of you to think the same thing. And I'm also always open to new ideas you might be able to bring to the discussion."

He referred back to the syllabus from the first class and noted that even though it was brief there would be a lot of information covered—including every single topic that was noted by each student that day. As the class progressed throughout the next ten weeks more questions would come up, and those too would be discussed.

"Your next assignment is to break out into two groups. Guys vs girls. These are the groups we will hold for the first half of class. Then, we will switch it up, and I will draw names from a hat. Yes, you heard right—a hat. It's still the best way to be fair in life, you know. You will meet anytime you'd like on any day you'd like to work on the assignment, but however you do it, find the time.

"Girls, you take the angle of the Bible; specifically the

books of Daniel, Revelation and end times prophecy from the Gospels of Matthew and Mark. Even if you aren't Christian, or if your belief system doesn't include any particular religion, I think this is something most Americans can relate to.

"Guys, you will look at end times from the science angle. Research everything 'non-religion' related. In a week you'll be presenting and debating on what you find. Don't worry. We will flip and do the opposite too. You'll find it to be competitive in who can *out research* the other team."

Mr. Harrison checked his watch and then dismissed the class but not before requesting one last thing. "Be open-minded. Remember this is a learning environment for all of us."

Before people even started to get up to leave, Indya called the girls to gather around. They joined her on the window side of the circle.

"Where were ya thinking we should meet? I'd say the library, since we'll need to research I guess. But I don't even know where the library is on this campus." Indya used her left index finger to scratch the back of her head.

Fiona was quick to respond. "No, not the library. Who goes to the library anymore?"

They all answered by simultaneously laughing. Even Mr. Harrison who was now packed to leave chuckled under his breath.

Ro had a suggestion. "How about Café Java? Everyone here drink coffee?"

There were a few nods.

Piper replied, "Oh yeah."

"And scones," Indya added.

Ro continued talking as they turned to leave. "Okay, let's plan for Saturday morning if that works for everyone. 10:00?"

"Before we go I wanted to formally introduce myself to you all. I'm Piper"

"And I'm Veronica, but please call me Ronny. My family and all my friends know me as Ronny, and from what Mr. Harrison says, we'll all get really close really fast in this class."

"As you know, I'm Ro, short for Rowena. It was my grandma's name."

Fiona cocked her head and shrugged. "I like it."

Indya was quick to add, "Me too. I'm a country for goodness sake and not even spelled the same way it should be. Talk about confusing to people."

They all laughed again, and with that the girls' group research party was set. Each left smiling and sharing secrets and ideas. It was a lot different than the look of class dismissal on that first day.

The guys had gathered in the hallway as soon as class was over. Other students began milling around, and they shifted their group to the corner by a stairwell.

Zane was the first to speak. "Let's get this over with. How about we meet at Shipman's Tavern down on Broad Street later this evening, maybe 6:00 or 7:00. They have two for one's tonight!"

"Yeah, that sounds perfect. I work the rest of the week," Ty added.

Ezra looked at Ty trying to figure out what his job was, and then said, "Sure, I can do that. Arch? You in?"

Arch fidgeted nervously with his backpack strap. "I don't know. Maybe it's not the best place to concentrate on the project. Plus...well, I don't drink."

Keno snorted at his response. "You don't have to get tanked. Yeah, it's a bar, but I'm sure they serve soda and water too."

"I just—I'm not comfortable."

Raising his eyebrows Keno was growing suspicious. "Seriously? Okay, well…"

Arch now had a red tint to his cheeks. He shook his head, and his dark hair flopped with the motion. "No, it's okay. I'll go."

Leo spoke up. "Dude, if he doesn't wanna meet there let's go somewhere else."

"Guys, I'm okay. Seriously. I'll be at Shipman's at 6:00."

4

Piper spoke for the girls. She explained how Christian Eschatology was mostly concerned with death; with what occurs before, after, and during it.

"This includes Heaven, Hell, the return of Jesus, and the resurrection of the dead," Piper explained. "And depending on your theological convictions, there is also a lot of discussion regarding the Rapture of the Saints and The Great Tribulation during the end times. The central event of the End of Days is the Second Coming of Christ. Until His return, death and suffering are the common lot of all people. Or as Jim Morrison once said, *No one gets out alive.* But in the end, and after a horrific ongoing struggle, good will triumph over evil.

Mr. Harrison was quick to follow up with a question. "But when will this all happen?"

Piper looked at her team mates, but when nobody spoke up, she answered. "No one knows. It's something Christians are living in expectation of, but the Bible offers no real date as to when Jesus will return."

Mr. Harrison followed up with another question. "So how do you prepare for such end times?"

Piper shrugged. "You live Christ-like and believe."

"Good start. Okay, gentleman. It's your turn."

Indya furrowed her eyebrows and shared glances at the other girls who who appeared equally confused. Was the *good start* for the work they did on the subject matter, or Piper's answer that living Christ-like was a good way to prepare for the End of Days? She was still running the thought through her head when Leo stood to represent the guys.

"Most of the research we found reflected Christian Eschatology," he said. "Which makes sense since this class is listed as a branch of theology. In a way it made our research harder because the field seems particularly well-defined by the Christian faith. But, on the other hand, since we only had to focus on a small area of study, there was less ground to cover.

"What we discovered was actually pretty interesting. Along with the disaster predictions that include everything from the sun exploding and volcanoes erupting, to black holes sucking the life off the planet. Other possible world-ending events involve natural disasters like global pandemics, and man-made disasters like nuclear wars and terrorism—acts that could cause the people on earth to literally kill themselves off."

Mr. Harrison nodded as if thinking of what to ask, then he linked his fingers in front of him and asked, "Do you believe it would take something as extreme as nuclear warfare to eliminate the world's population? Or could something small do the same thing?"

Leo shrugged his shoulders. "I don't know. What kind of small thing do you have in mind?"

"Taking away someone's right, maybe? Or losing a precious commodity or resource such as—well, let's say drinking water."

"Maybe, but I don't think something that small would have global implications. It might wipe out a local or regional population, but I don't thing it would be widespread." Leo wasn't convinced.

"No, I think it could, "Ro began to embrace Mr. Harrison's reasoning. "I think people would kill over certain things—to protect their families, or to gain power."

Arch joined in. "That's right. Look at the riots that break out when someone breaks the law or does something some-one else doesn't agree with. It's like a wildfire. Rage spreads like crazy when that happens."

Mr. Harrison nodded again, this time with more conviction, "Exactly. And if that kind of hysteria spreads, we could cause the world to end just as easily, if not easier, than a major natural disaster. Scary isn't it?"

5

Four weeks into class and the students began to realize how much they had to cover and the little time they had to do it in. Deep debates had filled most of the classes up to that point. Most of them had been fact-based from the research the teams had done. This included when each group had to flip sides and argue the reverse.

But the class started to develop a different feel from ordinary collage courses. Students were adding more of their own beliefs, values, ideas, and opinions into the conversations. Discussions grew based on upbringings and religious sectors, ranging from those who embraced a pre-millennial rapture theology, to those who thought Jesus would simply come again, versus those who were still on the fence about Revelation in general. They tossed around the concept of The Big Bang theory, evolution, and even aliens—although most of the class laughed that off as nonsense.

At times Mr. Harrison had to reel the groups in, calm them down, and redirect questions to ensure the discussions didn't degenerate into arguments, providing everyone the best environment possible for learning. He told them that within the few weeks left there would be time to get everyone's opinions on the table.

As the hushed conversation began to draw to a close that day Ezra asked, "Speaking of few weeks left, are we even going to have a final in this class?"

Mr. Harrison cracked his knuckles and folded his arms in front of him before continuing. "We will have a final *assignment*, yes. But it won't be your usual timed written exam. Instead, you will need to prove you've paid attention throughout the class. My goal is to have you walk out of here prepared."

Ezra looked up from his doodling. "Prepared?"

"With skills. With knowledge. Be able to tell others about what you did in here for the previous ten weeks. Maybe you'll be able to offer help to others."

"Sounds like *Survival of the Fittest*," Leo said, referring to the hot new reality TV show.

"In a way it is," Harrison replied. "If you think about the end of the world—maybe not in the sense of Jesus returning or the rapture, if that's what you believe in—think about instead of another civil war. You aren't going to just lie down and give up are you?"

Some shook their heads. Other voiced a tentative, "No."

"Ok, then so in that sense, yes, it's survival of the fittest. As far as Revelation and Jesus coming back—I'm a Christian, and I'm ready for it…" he trailed off.

"But that's not what you believe will happen is it?" Piper asked.

Swallowing, Mr. Harrison answered, "I don't think it's what we need to prepare for now."

"You mean you think before the Bible end of times… there is another end to worry about?"

"Yes."

A crowd in the hallway was growing louder. Class was over. The students filed out feeling there was so much more needed to be said.

6

M̲r. Harrison entered the classroom talking, which brought an end to conversations as everyone turned around and paid closer attention. "I want to start this class off today with a preface. I don't want to offend anyone nor change anyone's personal beliefs. I'm going to share my thoughts very quickly. Then I'm going to ask you to do something you probably won't understand, and might not want to do. Bear with me, though; it's all within good reason; at least as much reason as I believe.

"First, as I've already confessed, I am a Christian. I've said it before, and it's how I ended the last class. I've been a Christian all my life. But in addition to that I remember history class, as I'm sure you guys remember as well. This country was founded on God. In God we Trust is on our currency. Still, to this day. The Declaration of Independence was written in a house of God. Because of this I feel this country was born with our Father in heaven as the true leader of the nation. What I can't explain is when we truly started to go toward the polarizing opposite side. Instead of wanting to ask for help from Him, we as a country defied Him, said we could build stronger, lead better, and become a better nation apart from Him. For the most part it looked like it was working.

Other nations and people from all over the world looked on the USA with envy because of our prosperity. In actuality, we hurt ourselves, became morally corrupt and crippled. Eventually other countries began to despise and reject our country as a leader of nations."

The class nodded in agreement, looking like a bunch of bobbing-head toys.

Mr. Harrison continued, "So, now please turn your attention to the board."

Mr. Harrison wrote: *Say nothing. Ask no questions. TURN OFF and PLACE your phone or any electronic device you have on you in this box. Important: Please do both.* He underlined certain words for emphasis.

A few students silently mouthed, *What?* or *Why?* But no one spoke aloud. An ominous sense pervaded the room.

Harrison continued to write. *Trust me. I will explain after you do this one request.*

One by one every power button was pressed. Laptops, phones, and every other electronic device made their way into the box.

"I'll be right back," Mr. Harrison spoke then picked up the box and quickly exited the room.

There were quiet murmurs among the groups, but no one felt comfortable speaking above a whisper. By the time Harrison returned the class was full of conjectures about the professor's odd request.

"Ok," Harrison said as he walked into the classroom. "All of your items are safely stored in the trunk of my car."

Leo spoke loudly, "No way."

"Why?" Ro added.

Hr. Harrison was quick to explain. "Here's the thing. If

you don't take anything else away from this class; take this. Your phone, laptop, anything with an internet connection can monitor your every move. It can tell where you are, right? Your GPS? What about face recognition in social media apps? Or your banking apps? They keep your account secure, right? But what could someone who was less than scrupulous do with that information? I mean how did that advertiser who popped up the latest rod and reel know you were with your dad on a fishing boat on a Sunday afternoon? Is it possible that someone was listening on your conversations; tracking your movements; knowing what you purchased and how you paid for it?"

"Sounds like a conspiracy theory to me," Leo said.

Mr. Harrison smiled. "Does, doesn't it?"

Zane leaned back in his chair crossing his arms as he spoke. "But it also sounds pretty freakin' legit to me. Never thought of that."

Some added, "Me either."

Another one said, "Dang! Big Brother is listening."

Mr. Harrison leaned back at his usual spot on the window sill and nodded. "Now the explanation for my strange request, although you've probably already guessed. You'll get all your belongings back at the end of class. But until then, and for the rest of class, we will talk… Well, I guess you could say about conspiracy theory. I want to be very honest with you, and that's why I gave you full disclosure in the beginning of class. I have an opinion—as do all of you. I may change your opinion, although I'm really not trying to. This is how I feel. This is what I believe. And I pray I'm wrong."

7

"So, Mr. Harrison, speaking of conspiracy theory, I saw something on TV about Federal Freedom Camps. They are designed to help the citizens…" Ezra trailed off.

Mr. Harrison shook his head, slowly at first and then with more effort.

This was the answer Ezra needed, and he nodded. "Thought so."

"You mean they don't *help* us?" Ro asked with apparent shock crossing her face.

"Let's just say you don't always need to believe what you hear, or trust the people that are put in place to lead you."

"I'm a sitting duck then, because I didn't know anything. If they came knocking at my door I'd get on the bus."

Leo was quick to add, "Literally. That's probably how they will operate… just come and pick people up if it comes down to it."

Ro gasped, "Unbelievable."

Looking at his watch, Mr. Harrison closed the discussion. "Well, okay. I can't believe we're already out of time for today. When you leave I want you to do some more research. Remember, though, if you look into too much, search online, watch videos—if you leave a pattern, you could be flagged.

Companies are not supposed to track you, but I don't know the accuracy in that. I don't trust that I have—that any of us have—much privacy anymore. Just be aware that if you leave a trail it could show a pattern which draws attention."

The debate and conversation that the class had brought that day had been the most intense to date. There were moments of shock, disbelief, frustration, and anger. There were laughs, minutes of complete silence, and some students, including Piper and Fiona, were reduced to tears.

Mr. Harrison had spent years accumulating data he believed showed how the nation would eventually fall from its own excesses. He made a convincing argument that history can repeat itself, drawing on information from government manuals to history books and especially the Bible. He explained how scientists showed indescribable scenarios of natural, political, and economic collapse, and noted that both Christian and secular scholars alike agreed. He showed where details were unfolding that made people questioned the truth of what they were seeing on television, from the news media, and even from official government sources. With the rise of misinformation, people didn't know who to trust anymore.

"It doesn't take a rocket scientist," he mused. "Even a child can see this place is going to hell in a handbasket. The only question is, how fast are we going to get there, and who's going along for the ride.

"The economy is fractured. No surprise there. Many of you mentioned that in your last group assignments. Think of it this way: A kid falls off a bike and breaks his arm. He gets a cast, his arm is in a sling for a few weeks, and before you know it he's back to riding the same bike, climbing trees, or swimming—doing all the things he was doing before the accident. Then he does it again. But this time it takes more than a few weeks to heal, because more damage was done to the already damaged bone. Now imagine that poor kid breaking and re-breaking that same bone multiple times, over and over again. Eventually it won't heal itself anymore. There's just not enough left of the original bone to be salvaged. That's our dollar. It's no longer worth the pretty paper it's printed on."

"If that's the case, what are we supposed to do with our currency?" Ty asked quietly.

Mr. Harrison walked the edge of the room and stared out the windows for a long moment before answering. "You'd be better off starting a fire with it. You'd get more use out of it that way."

A recent international studies class lecture came to Keno's mind. "China owns a lot of U.S. Treasury bonds. We are indebted to them big time. What happens if they no longer support our dollar? If they no longer support us as a country?"

A chill ran through the entire class.

Mr. Harrison fixed him with a stare. "If China calls in their loans to this country, our economy will collapse," he said. "As a country, we'd be doomed."

Keno's eyes grew wide with his next thought. *We are doomed.*

8

After leaving class that day there was an odd silence among the groups. Nobody wanted to speak for fear of what might be overheard—and by whom. Eventually Ro swallowed hard and spoke first. "I'm afraid to do anything. I don't even want to talk on my phone now."

Ty stopped walking and waited for her to catch up, "I don't think that's what Mr. Harrison is talking about. Not what he wants at all actually. We're *supposed* to research. We aren't supposed to be scared."

Indya shook her head. "Speak for yourself. That just got real man."

Zane was quick to also add. "Probably means don't look up anything that would land you in jail or on America's Most Wanted list.

Piper sighed and tugged her backpack tight on her shoulders. "You know, I don't even want to talk to anyone else about it. I don't mind the research, but I'm afraid of what others would say if I tried to ask for their opinions."

"Yeah Dawson and I fought last night because of this class."

"What do you mean, Ro?" Piper gently touched her arm.

"He said Mr. Harrison is a quack and needs to stop teaching everyone such B.S."

It was Ronny that spoke up next. "Did you tell Dawson what we're talking about? What does he say about all of this end-of-the-world stuff?"

"He says he's an Econ major; that there is nothing this country is going through that we won't survive, and he's tired of people saying otherwise. He says that they don't know what they're talking about because they aren't knowledgeable enough, and that *we* aren't knowledgeable enough."

Zane turned to face Ro. He scratched through his stiff-styled blond hair and huffed. "So your boyfriend called you stupid—*us* stupid."

"No. He just—"

"Yes, he called us stupid. If you aren't knowledgeable, then you're stupid."

Ro defended Dawson by saying, "More like uneducated."

He was now getting angry. "Same difference!"

"You know what, it doesn't matter. He won't listen to anything I say about the class anyway, so I just won't talk about it with him anymore."

"Sounds like a great guy."

"Zane you don't know him. Plus, it doesn't matter. After what we've been learning in class, I don't think I'll have time to find out who Dawson really is. And he certainly won't make time to share with me. Anyway, I gotta go. I have to be somewhere."

Ronny was holding Zane's arm in a firm grasp. "I can't believe you just said that. What does it matter to you what some guy you don't know says anyway?"

"It doesn't. I just think the guy sounds like an arrogant barbarian. I don't deal well with that kind."

She ran the pad of her thumb around his bicep. "It's not

your battle to fight. And keep an open mind. Remember what Mr. Harrison said."

"I do, but obviously this Dawson joker can't do that or doesn't have a mind to keep open."

The rest of the group broke up and went in separate directions. Ronny just shook her head. She was beginning to wonder why she was with an arrogant barbarian herself.

9

The rumble of conversation around the room was interrupted when Mr. Harrison took his usual spot along the windowsill and raised his voice. "Remember what we ended with yesterday?" A hush slowly fell on the room as he caught attention of each person, and they acknowledged his question, understanding its deeper meaning—*Nobody should say anything of defiance.* "Today, then, we'll discuss Martial Law."

When the room was in complete silence he continued. "Now I don't want to scare anyone, but this is something that has happened in other countries and can certainly happen here in this one again."

"Again?" Fiona questioned.

"Yes—martial law is something that's been imposed during the revolutionary and Civil wars and on a few other occasions. So who can tell me what it is exactly?"

Nobody spoke for a few seconds. Arch scanned the room and then quietly spoke up. "Martial Law is something the president or government official in charge would call for in time of war, maybe civil war or natural disaster. It would be done to prevent civil unrest and is designed to protect citizens."

"What happens to those who don't follow it," Mr. Harrison asked.

"They'd be court martialed."

Mr. Harrison continued to describe how other countries had faced martial law and the effects it had on their citizens. The class appeared to listen, but he could tell the message was not really being absorbed. There were even a few yawns and some doodling going on among the students, so he asked a follow-up question he knew would spark discussion. "Specifically, what could that mean for the United States?"

This time Arch remained quiet, eyes focused back to the instructor

Mr. Harrison continued. "Aside from mandatory curfew, one of the biggest effects martial law would have on the United States is the suspension of Habeas Corpus. Do you know what Habeas Corpus is?"

"Sounds like something to do with death," Zane burst out.

Ronny looked at him. "You *would* think that, wouldn't you?"

Mr. Harrison ignored them and continued. "It's actually a right given to every American citizen. To me. To you. It's the right of every prisoner to challenge the terms of his or her incarceration while in court."

Ro raised her hand. "So like, *you have the right to remain silent?*"

Mr. Harrison smiled. "That's Miranda Rights. That would happen *before* the court visit."

The class burst out in laughter. Even Ro joined in.

The rest of the lecture and discussion was kept to history lessons and generalizations. Nothing was said that would cause alarm or draw attention to them. Mr. Harrison smiled and bid everyone a good evening as he handed each person a paper on the way out. It read:

Your Next Assignment

Your groups are listed at the top. By next class, meet up with everyone on your respective teams. There is a lot of work to do and not much time left to do it in."

Ty thought the assignment referred to classwork, but he couldn't help but think Harrison meant more than the note said.

10

The title on top of the page read, Bug-out bags.

"Sounds disgusting," Ro made a show of poking her finger down her throat in the universal *gag-me* symbol as she read the assignment aloud.

"It's not really about insects, Ro." Ronny laughed, then added, "At least I don't think it is."

Ro continued to recite from the page. "Something you would take on your person if it's the only thing you can grab in an emergency. Be that a backpack, suitcase, or even pillow case. What would you put in there to allow you to survive in a disaster or other emergency situation? Think outside the box, or should I say, bag."

"His humor never gets old," Arch interrupted.

Ro smiled at Arch and continued reading. "As you work on the list, explain why some things are left off, what makes certain things necessary, and others only desirable to have?"

The group sat around the table looking at one another for someone to start. Ty was first to speak. "First you need the bag; the container—whatever you're going to use to hold all your stuff. I'd say, let's choose a backpack. Makes the most sense, right? Then we need to list the things that we must have to live."

Ezra, who rounded out the first of the two groups, started ticking items off on his fingers. "Yeah, food, water, shelter, fire, and security."

"And don't forget, we need to think about what would actually fit in a backpack," Arch noted.

"Perfect!" Ro squeaked. "Now let's start listing."

They began to brainstorm, and Ro wrote down the ideas as they were called out. In the end they had three times the amount of stuff that could possible fit into a standard backpack, and started the challenging task of prioritizing and eliminating items. Arguments on what constituted a want versus what was a true need ensued. Finally, after much discussion and heated debate, the group finished, and Ro dropped her pencil and massaged her cramping fingers. They agreed that even though not ideal, the list of items would hopefully enable them to survive a catastrophe.

"I wonder how the other group is doing?" Ezra said as they were disbursing.

"They have Leo on their team, so probably pretty good," Ty commented.

Ronny made a disappointing grunt. "You're right. How would we ever compete?"

Arch stopped ahead of the group and turned to face them. "We don't," he said. "This isn't a competition. Haven't you learned anything from the other assignments we've done? This isn't a winner-take-all class; this is a learning experience. Mr. Harrison is preparing us. I don't know why, but I don't think this is about getting an A in the class. I think Harrison is preparing us to make the best possible decisions for a worst case scenario."

11

Leo's group had come to class with a very detailed list, including a drawing of the tactical bag used featuring carabineers lining the outside with everything from flashlight to tin cup hooked on the bag. Mr Harrison was impressed, and even gave the group a slow clap.

"Why didn't we think of that?" Ro whispered to Ronny.

"It's okay. We got some magic of our own," Ronny reminded her.

Mr. Harrison interrupted their hushed conversation. "As before, go ahead and mark off those items on your list that the first group notes. Then we'll see what is left on the second team's list. The assignment was to list important items you need to survive. How'd you do? Was it easy?"

Ezra spoke up. "Too easy. We ended up with so much we'd need a truck and trailer to haul it around."

"Were you able to narrow it down?"

Ronny answered for the team. "Yeah, but not everyone was happy about it."

Mr. Harrison chuckled. "Isn't that how all good debates go?" He then pointed to the left side of the circle. "Okay, Leo, since you brought the visual aid, your group is up first."

Between the two groups items were checked and crossed

off. The reasoning for allowing each accepted item on the essential list kept the group discussion going for most of the class. Finally Mr. Harrison asked, "Is there anything we're missing here?"

"Yeah," Zane spoke up. "Cash."

Arch laughed. Leo joined in.

"Why are you laughing?" Zane's reaction was somewhere between embarrassment and anger.

Arch answered more boldly than usual. "Cash won't count anymore. People, listen. It's like we talked about in class before. In the aftermath, a dollar bill will be just another piece of paper. It will no longer have value. Seems impossible right now, but in the end it isn't."

Leo added, "Once a detail like that hits the news, it will be too late. Pandemonium will ensue. It will be utter chaos. Murders, theft, rapes. I can't even imagine what people would do to get what they need for their families."

"And you wanna be in the middle of all that?" Piper looked at Zane who sat in confused silence.

Keno huffed from his right, "Not me man. Get me the hell outta here if it hits the fan."

Mr. Harrison now spoke. "That's why you need to be prepared. To have a plan."

"So... if no cash then what?" Zane was slowly coming to the realization on what was being said.

"Instead you need to have things to barter with at all times. Barter, trading goods for services—or goods for different kinds of goods—will be the key to survival." Mr. Harrison crossed his arms. "And if you don't have things to barter, you'd better have skills or the ability to do work needed in exchange for what you require."

For the remainder of class the discussion turned into more end of times survival training. Who will bring what to the table? It was determined that everyone has skills, and if nothing else they have ideas. The more they talked about current events, the more they concluded that they might just be living in the precursor to the 'final events' time.

"Class, before we get out of here, I have a question for you," Mr. Harrison said. "Can anyone tell me happened yesterday afternoon?"

Someone in the room muttered, "I don't know."

"With the stock market?" Harrison hinted.

Looks of confusion swarmed the circle. No answers were voiced. Finally Fiona said, "Nobody watches the news, Mr. Harrison."

A smattering of laughter followed, and Indya added, "We get all our news from social media."

Instead of commenting on the questionable accuracy of social media fact checkers, Mr. Harrison looked in the direction where Arch sat with his arms crossed and a grim look on his face. He nodded, knowing the answer. "The stock market tanked. Literally. It fell so hard and fast the newscasters, investors, pretty much everyone was caught off guard."

Zane was quick to respond. "It will bounce back. It always has."

Mr. Harrison took a second, nodded, and blinked a few times, "Maybe. But what if it doesn't?"

Ronny whispered, "Black Tuesday. That's what they called the stock market collapse that started the Great Depression. If the stock market crashes, it could begin a domino-effect resulting in a major economic collapse. Businesses fail. People out of work. Shortages of basic necessities. It has happened in the past."

"Exactly. So, what should be our response?"

"I guess we need to do what you've suggested all along. Be prepared," Arch answered just as quietly as Ronny had.

Mr. Harrison addressed Indya's comment regarding the dependence on social media. "What do you usually see come across your feeds?"

Everyone starting shouting out answers at once:

"People complaining."

"Funny cat videos."

"Pictures of food.

"Michael Jackson memes."

"Everyone being offended by everything."

"Ah!" Mr. Harrison stopped them. "That is what I was hoping to get at. Have you noticed that people seem to get offended so much easier these days?"

Keno spoke up. "Oh yeah, doesn't matter race, gender, sexual orientation, or even the time of the day, someone will always be offended."

"And doesn't if feel like it's being shoved down your throats?"

"Yes."

Mr. Harrison nodded. "Well it is. Or at least that is another conspiracy theory. Things can be fed and spread to anyone with internet access. As you said, that is the source people go to for news today. In our current online environment, a piece of information can spread like wildfire, regardless of whether that information is true or false."

Time ran, and Mr. Harrison dismissed the class with a final suggestion. "You might want to keep these lists—you know, just in case."

Piper stayed in her seat remembering something she read during her group research when she was studying the

Christian view Eschatology. She paged back through her sketchy notes until she found what she was looking for and re-read them to herself.

End Time Prophecies: History repeats itself. The final judgment of God will reveal what 'man' has' done in relation to God and His people. The essence of human history—battle between good and evil. Between God and Satan. Are we in a spiritual battle? Yes. Good news: Each time of testing brought the total defeat of God's enemies. Christ-centered war as the climax of salvation history.

She looked up, caught Mr. Harrison's eye, and asked, "We are in a Christ-centered war, aren't we?"

He only had to nod his head to give her the confirmation she already had.

12

I t was the next to last lecture for the Eschatology class, and Mr. Harrison was late. He was also distracted. The class watched as he quickly walked to the desk and placed his backpack loudly in its usual spot. He ripped the zipper open and paged through files inside. He stopped, looked out the window for a few seconds as if thinking of something before continuing. Then, as if remembering where he put the file, he nodded once and closed the bag.

"Sorry I'm late guys, just needed to get some stuff together. How is everyone? Before anyone could answer he continued. "We've learned so much in here that I want everyone to take 10-20 minutes to list things that you can walk away from this class with—information you know today that you didn't know 10 weeks ago."

As everyone went to work on their lists, Mr. Harrison pulled out his phone and began punching texts rapidly to an unknown recipient. The clicking of his keyboard sounds droned on for the next 25 minutes until he realized the time and finally set the phone down. He then asked each student, one by one, to read aloud their lists.

"As we did with the bug-out bag lists, mark off as each person says something that's on your list. We'll see how many we come up with. If as a group you have 50 or more items you all pass with an A. 40—you each get a B. 30—a C and so forth."

Gasps encircled the class as people started to count their lines from their papers in their head.

"You all sound scared. I never told you to put your pencils down. You can still add to your list. No worries. I know you all have this. This is a team effort. So, as a team let's get you all 'A's. And you have until the end of class to get there."

Upon dismissal that day Mr. Harrison was quite sincere in his send offs. He encouraged everyone to be careful and that God willing they'd be back there same time, same place for the last class. "With the final out of way, we can plan to have open dialogue on any topic that was covered."

God willing? Ro thought. *That seems an odd thing to say.*

Everyone shrugged it off and said their goodbyes. Most had other final exams to prepare. But as these preparations went on, events were transpiring in the background. The stock market continued to fall, slowly but steadily, as it had every day since the bug-out bag assignment was made. Other students and professors on campus, aside from Mr. Harrison, were too distracted with the demands of life to see it—the grades, the finals, the place they'd fall in the hierarchy of grade point averages.

It's those everyday distractions that catch even the smartest person off guard, Harrison thought.

13

I t is just after 2:30 that Thursday afternoon. The message that Arch sent to everyone in class said:

'Meet in commons 4:00!!

Most arrived early with Keno and Leo straggling in 4:02. Keno was the only one to ask why they were there. Arch didn't answer. Instead he silently pulled out his cellphone and signaled without talking for everyone to turn their electronics off, mimicking Mr. Harrison's actions during class. He then deposited his phone into a shoebox that he held out in front and motioned with his head for everyone else to do the same.

They hesitated.

"No. What for?" Keno asked.

Indya followed his question by saying she didn't understand.

Piper just shrugged an *I'm doing it,* turned off her phone, deposited it into the box, and slid her hands into the back pockets of her jeans.

Arch remained silent, holding the box each until person followed Piper and added their phones. He held up a finger and then walked away. The group watched as he put the box into the trunk of his car which sat about 60 yards away.

Once he returned he immediately went into detail confessing that he spent a sad majority of his time listening to an old ham radio with his great-uncle. That morning they overheard talk about troops moving in and preparing for *Plan 21D*.

Confusion painted the faces of everyone around him.

Ro was quick to ask. "What does that mean? And how do you know all of this. I don't remember talking about it in class."

"Look, I don't have time to explain this. I don't understand what that means either," he confessed. "But we distinctly heard the term, Martial Law, mentioned, and a woman repeated it back and said, "Affirmed." They didn't say anything about suspending the right of habeas corpus, but the guy they referred to as *General* did order them to initiate the "Suspension Clause," whatever that is."

Arch swallowed hard and confessed. "Okay, so this class meant something more to me than a grade. I've assumed something big was coming down the pike for a long time now. I've spent the past couple of years doing research on the US and the path this country was heading toward. But I needed to get outside of my own head, you know what I mean? I needed to get a better understanding of what it all means from someone who seemed to actually know what they were talking about. And—well—I needed an elective. This class seemed to check all the boxes. I just didn't think it would happen so soon."

Ezra shook his head as if to clear the confusion before speaking, "Wait. What does Mr. Harrison say? Did you even talk to him about this?"

Arch was stoic. "Where do you think I just came from?"

Zane walked closer into the circle. "Did *he* say it's time?"
Arch nodded.

"Where is he now then?" Keno asked.

"He's preparing—getting things ready for his family. I told him I'd leave a note letting him know where we are."

"So where will that be? What do we do?" Zane was beginning to sound anxious.

Piper was quick to answer. "We go. We use what we've learned, and we leave."

Indya threw her backpack to the ground and frantically unzipped the bag digging through the contents. She looked through some papers before pulling out her checklist. It wasn't ideal. Most of the original items on the list had been scratched through. New additional items had been jotted down as quickly as people had spoken, some were nearly illegible. But it was a start. As she read the notes out loud, others started throwing out suggestions.

"Hold up, guys. First things first. Where do we go?" Ty's voice was shaky.

Arch supplied the answer. "My grandparents have land. It's been in the family for generations. There's a small hunting cabin on it a few miles from Lake Potter. It sits in the valley surrounded by mountains, and there is a creek on the property for fresh water, although we'll want to boil it to kill any parasites. It's rustic, but it's better than sleeping in tents—or worse, facing Freedom camps. My older brother Seth and dad used to go hunting there years ago... before Seth passed away. Then we all stopped going there. I haven't been there in years."

Sidetracked, Ronny stopped him. "Your brother died? I didn't know that I'm sorry."

"Yeah, I'm sorry too. There's a lot you didn't know about me. Bottom line: I have a key. I don't know what we'll see when we get there, but it's a place to go. And it's off the grid." Arch flashed a dull gold key.

Nerves coated the words Ro said next. "I don't know. I don't think I can leave. I can't—I can't just..."

"Yeah, I mean what if what you heard was wrong. What if nothing happens?" It was Zane who interrupted that time.

"Let's say we're wrong. Look at it as a vacation, a camping trip for a long weekend," Ty suggested as he ran a hand through his short blond hair.

"During finals week? This is such a stupid idea." Ezra didn't hide the concern he had.

"Mr. Harrison will know where we are. Anyway, we all did our final assignment for the class, right? So that final is done."

"Or maybe this *is* the final, and surviving it will tell us if we pass or not."

"Not funny, Keno. And that's not what I mean. Some of us have other finals, you know," Ronny said as she rolled her eyes.

"You don't have to come with us. You can stay here with your *boyfriend*." Keno air-quoted. He was now getting defensive.

"Don't you dare—" Zane started.

Ronny was quick to stop him. "Yes, I do," she shot back at Keno.

Keno held his ground. "Why? There are lots of people staying here. Nobody else seems to think there's anything worry about. Why not just stay here with them and study for your finals?"

"Why? *Why*? Because you're right! Because *we're* right. And I don't want to be with them and be wrong."

14

Leo reigned the group back in. "Ok, we don't have time to fight. We have shelter. But we don't even know what kind of condition that place is in. Do you know Arch? I just hope it's in good condition."

"Me too, but it doesn't matter. We'll make do with what is there," Arch assured him.

"Let's break up into groups to get supplies. What's next on the list?" Leo asked after taking the list from Indya. "We need to be the most efficient with the little time that we have.

"How much time is that?" she asked.

"I don't know exactly, but let's assume not a lot. I suggest we break into groups of two or three," Leo said and then read down the list. "First is food. Who can be the quickest in a grocery store? I would say food is the most important segment, but honestly, we're talking about survival here. Every segment is equally important."

Piper and Ro both raised their hands.

"Good," he said. "The heaviest load will likely be drinking water. Who has a truck?'"

Zane raised a hand.

"We'll get the water," said Ronny

"The hardest to come by might be weapons and

ammunition. Anyone live around here and have an arsenal?" he quipped.

Ty nodded. "I may not have an arsenal like the National Guard Armory, but I like to hunt. I've got a bow and arrows, and we have a few guns at my place."

"Ezra don't you have some too? I thought you mentioned that you did some dear hunting," Indya asked, looking in his direction.

Ezra nodded. "And I can get additional ammo and survival gear at the sporting goods store."

"Good. Now, heat and fire."

Keno looked at Leo, and they silently agreed. Then he asked, "Should we get a bunch of wood?"

Leo shook his head. "We will be in the forest, so wood's not a problem. But we need things to make fire and to cook with. Think backwoods camping but long term. It's more like flint and steel than matches and lighter fluid."

Keno nodded in agreement.

"Arch and Fiona, would you like to get the items needed for health?"

"Sure," they said in unison.

Ronny asked the question everyone was thinking. "Where do we go when we're done?"

Arch spoke up. "We meet back in that parking lot in two hours. I know that's not much time. If you're late I'll leave you an address on that light pole, but you need to figure out how to get there—*without* your phones or GPS. This is off-grid time. We don't want anyone tracking us. That means everyone pick up a map of the state while you're out. The fact is, we don't know where we might be walking to in the coming days—or weeks."

"Or months," Leo added.

A somber pall settled over the group as the weight of Leo's comment pressed down on them.

Arch blew out a breath, checked his watch, and said, "We will pull out of here no later than 6:30. Eat your favorite fast food on the way here. It might be the last time you have it in a while."

By now Ro was in tears, and Piper looked like she was going to be sick. Zane was upset that he still stood there listening to the garbage people said. Ronny was wide-eyed, silently pleading with him to come. She tried to take his arm, but he jerked it away and mumbled, "Fine, I'll play along. But I'll be back by Monday."

Ezra overheard the exchange and commented, "Yeah, treat it as a practice run, a mini-vacation. It'll be cool."

Indya asked, "Who is paying for all of this stuff? I mean you can't expect us to go buy handguns, right?"

"No time for that, and I'm not sure we want to be on anyone's radar for suddenly buying firearms. Think of alternative weapons like blow guns, pellet guns, sling shots. We'll see what they have at the sporting goods store when we get there," Ty said.

Fiona gripped her crossbody purse as if for encouragement. "The food and medicines will be the most expensive. I don't mind paying for the medications. My parents gave me a credit card for college and have yet to ask about what I buy."

Ro wiped away tears and said, "I guess I can do the same with my card."

"Water's cheap. We just need to buy a bunch of jugs and and can fill them from the tap at home," Ronny added.

Leo smiled. "See, this is the teamwork I'm talking about."

Ty looked at his watch. "We don't have a lot of time."

"You're right, we gotta get going. But remember you cannot tell anyone where we are going. Not *anyone*." Arch's demeanor shifted into something the group had never witnessed in him before—stern,

"That's not gonna happen. I have to tell my family." Ronny was adamant.

He shook his head. "You don't understand. We need to be hiding. Gone. If you have time within the two hours, go see them in person."

Keno raised his voice as he spoke. "Yeah, but that's not an option for most of us. We're states apart."

Arch put a hand on his shoulder and looked him in the eyes. "I understand. Best thing you can do is get a quick message to them that you'll be offline for a while. Tell them that you're going on a camping trip with some friends. It's not a lie. It's just not the whole truth."

Keno nodded reluctantly,.

Fiona allowed her gaze to wander over the commons. Life looked pretty normal to her. There were couples kissing and making small talk. Some girls were sitting in a circle under a tree, laughing as if they didn't have a care in the world. A group of sophomores had started a football game to the right of where they stood. Two other girls were laying on a blanket, reading in the sun. Others listen to music or talked among themselves. It was just like any other day on campus. How could they not know that their world was about to change forever?

"What about all of them?" she said. Everyone in the group turned to face her. Shouldn't we warn them?"

"Who?"

She motioned to the crowd around her with a sweep of her arm. "Everyone. We have to warn as many people as we can."

Arch spoke. "Didn't we all already try that? I mean, how many of us talked about this with our families, friends, even other classmates? They all called us crazy. Do you really think they'll believe us now?"

"Guys, come on. We have too much to do. We can tell them after, give them time to make up their minds one last time." Leo was dancing around nervously, ready to spring into action.

With the intentions of warning everyone when they returned, Fiona reluctantly followed the group to Arch's car to retrieve her phone from his trunk. They had less than two hours to get everything they needed before they had to bug-out.

15

"Why are we stopping here?" Ro asked noticing the Co-op sign as Piper pulled into a small parking lot.

"I'll be right back." She put the car in park, left it running, and ran inside through an open garage door.

Within a few minutes she returned carrying a big box that she slid into the back seat. She shut the door and ran back inside. From the backseat Ro heard the distinct sound of chirping.

This time Piper came back out with a roll of wire and three brown bags—one large and two that were smaller. She deposited it all on the other side of the back seat, and ran around to the driver's side, jumped in, moved the gear into reverse, and backing out as quickly as she had pulled in.

"There are 20 chicks, some chicken wire, and scratch feed," she said before Ro could ask the question.

"Ah, how cute," Ro commented. "But what are you gonna do with them?"

"Raise them."

"As pets?"

"No. As food. Some will lay eggs. Some will eventually be our dinner."

"Gross."

"Survival of the fittest. But you're right. They are cute."

"Gross again."

"I also picked up this." She handed a bag to Ro, who looked carefully inside. There were two vials and a plastic bag with a syringe and needles."

"What the heck? Drugs?" Ro started.

"Antibiotics."

"Antibiotics? They sell those here? I mean, don't you need a perscription or something?"

Piper shook her head. "Not when you're buying them for animals."

"Oh, so it's in case the chicks get sick."

"No. It's in case one of us does."

Ro made a face. "This day just keeps getting better and better."

"I know. In all seriousness, we only have an hour and a half now, and we've barely made a dent in our list."

The two began to discuss what store they should go to for their food items. The super store was closest, but it also had the worst crowds at check out. On the other hand they had the most stuff and better variety than the market across town.

"Super store it is," Ro said.

Piper pulled into the parking lot and spoke fast. "Let's plan on a slow checkout before going inside. We just need to be faster. Check the time. We only have an hour in here. No more. I will meet you at the front before that hour is up. Remember, we're not shopping—we're buying. We don't need to be going up and down every aisle in the store. In fact, quick, get a piece of paper while I park."

Ro grabbed an envelope from her purse and tested a pen. "Okay, shoot," she said.

"Rice and Beans."

"Like from New Orleans?" Ro asked while hurriedly writing.

"No, like dried beans and bags of uncooked rice."

"Ew? I can't imagine that being good. I mean I like rice okay, but that doesn't seem very appetizing." Ro said.

"It's not. At least, not without spices. But it's the food we will need for sustenance."

"Fine. Can we get spices?"

Piper sat with her purse on her lap and hand poised on the handle as if to jump out before catching fire. "Yes. Add it to the list. And powdered milk, oatmeal—and baking ingredients like flour and sugar. And salt. Lots of salt.

"Really?"

"Yeah, your body needs salt to live. Plus with sugar and salt you can cure meat. Remember, Leo and Ty were talking about that one day?"

"What about jerky or that type of meat?"

"Yeah, but it will need to be either dried or and canned. Stuff like canned tuna and chicken, veggies, soups, that kind of stuff. Stay away from anything that needs to be frozen or refrigerated. There's a pretty good chance we won't have electricity, so no refrigerator. We could use noodles too—dried or canned. Okay, we're burning daylight. We need to be done shopping within 45 minutes. Each of us gets a cart. I'll start in the back. You take the the front. When we're full, we're done. Oh, and don't stock up on bread. It will only go bad."

Ro stopped with her pen above the paper. "I will need coffee."

"Okay. Get some coffee."

"Do they even have stuff to cook with at the cabin?"

Piper opened the door, "I don't know. That's a good question. Get a pan or two if you see them, I'll get some heavy duty plastic cups and utensils. We can always wash them. Think of it like when we moved into the dorms. What did we need?"

"Paper towels. And toilet paper. Gotta have toilet paper. That's non-negotiable."

Ro joined Piper outside the car, and they walked quickly inside.

"Yes. I guess. But remember, disposable can't be replaced. Once it's gone, it's gone forever."

"Okay, then we need real towels and wash cloths. And soap to wash them."

"Uh huh."

"But I'm still getting toilet paper. Lots of toilet paper."

Piper nodded.

Once inside each grabbed a cart and took off silently but quickly in opposite directions. In the oatmeal aisle Piper picked up cereal bowls with cartoon characters. She added everything she remembered telling Ro from the list and made it completely back to the front of the store before running across Ro already in the checkout lane.

"Did you think of anything we forgot?" she asked.

Ro pointed to the top of the tower of items in her cart. "Feminine products. You girls can thank me later."

"Looks like more than tampons in there to me." Piper counted at least eight packages of ivory soap bars. "Why ivory soap?"

"I don't know. They had 10 bars in each package. More for the money. Who cares—it's soap, and soap is soap."

"And deodorants of every scent? Toothpaste and tooth brushes?"

"And cheap razors," Ro noted. "I also swiped across an

endcap of discontinued two-in-one kid's shampoo and conditioner for 89 cents each. I don't think anyone's gonna care as long as they have something to clean their hair with. Besides, I felt like I was on a shopping spree. I was already in that section, and I still had room in the cart. I didn't want to leave here knowing I could have gotten more."

Piper looked at her watch trying to figure out how much time they had left, as the cashier made small talk and took her time checking out the customer ahead of them in line.

"Com'on, com'on, com'on," she breathed. "We need to get out of here before we get left behind. By the time we get checked out, we'll be lucky to have 20 minutes to get back to the rendezvous point."

Ro stood in the lane beside Piper when a thought crossed her mind. "What if nothing happens?" she asked. "What are we going to do with all of this food? I certainly can't eat all those beans and rice."

Piper shrugged. "Feeling charitable?"

16

Everyone sat paired in cars waiting for the group to reconvene in the vacant parking lot at the east end of the campus. Except when there was a university sporting event, that particular lot usually stayed empty. Today, one by one, cars carrying class members joined together in parade-fashion.

It was the first day of finals week, but the world as they knew it had changed—at least from their perspectives. The halls and dorms at the university were bustling with activity. There would be lonely corners where people were cramming for tests. Every laptop would be open; notes would be reviewed and re-reviewed; books would be studied. Students fell into two categories; those who quietly roamed the halls in anxious anticipation of what would be on the exams to come and those excitedly getting ready to leave for the summer, glad the testing was finally done. And there was a third group; the group that didn't show up for their final exam. Or perhaps, by not showing up, they were taking their final exam. In any case, when the university's students into their classrooms for finals that day, there would be one room that was empty.

They got out before it was too late. They were gathered in the lonely, abandoned parking lot.

"She said she'd be right back," Piper said through her open window when asked where Fiona had run off to.

Arch looked again at his watch impatiently. He had just taped the note to the pole as he told Mr. Harrision that he'd do letting them know where they went. It was hidden under a power box with a hinged lid, unknown to anyone just walking by. This is also where he planned to leave instructions for the other classmates. He didn't have to. Everyone was back in time. Everyone except Fiona.

He tapped his watch face for emphasis. "We *have* to go."

Just then, as if on cue, a shower of papers flew from the second story balcony of the main hall. The wind caught the waterfall of white and carried the individual sheets of copied paper across the campus. Seconds later Fiona was running toward the group. Arch jumped in the car, and the caravan started to move in one long, snake-like wave of motion. She hopped in the front seat beside him.

She had done what she said she wanted. She sent a warning to everyone before they left.

Zane and Ronny drove third in line behind Arch and Fiona and Piper and Ro. In the rear view mirror Zane watched as confused people picked up and read the papers, some looking after the cars as they quickly drove away.

Ronny, beside him, was on the phone making an anxious call to her family. "I just think it's a good idea for you guys to be prepared for the worst. I don't know where we're going. I'll let you know when we get—"

The cell phone service went dead.

Ronny looked at Zane with confusion. "Cell towers are

down," he muttered. "Harrison said that would be the the first sign that it's happening. They—whoever *they* are—control communications. We're on our own now. No way to communicate with the outside world.

Zane suddenly remembered the last thing they were to do as they drove away. He grabbed Ronny's cell phone and threw it out the window leaving Ronny staring in disbelief.

17

"Yeah, this place definitely hasn't hasn't seen a human occupant in many years." Arch ran a hand over his damp forehead and through his hair. "I don't know what we'll find when we get inside." He noted the vines that cascaded over the porch and created an effective barrier across the front door and windows. there. "If we can get in there."

"Nothing a little knife won't fix," Leo grinned as he sauntered toward the cabin. He pulled out his machete as if he carried the monstrous blade with him wherever he went. He approached the steps like Indiana Jones in search of a priceless historical artifact. The top step cracked as he put his weight on it, and the front section splinted off into pieces. He stumbled backward a bit, then caught his balance and carefully tested the rest of the steps as he ascended onto the porch.

"Before we take anything out of the cars, we need to see what's in there. We can do inventory of all the stuff we all got once we figure out a place to put it."

Ty pulled vines out of the way as Leo cut a path. A few swipes of the machete and the decrepit screen door suddenly appeared. It was in relatively good shape considering the time it been left to the elements. Two of its three hinges

59

still held, and it awkwardly bounced along the porch as it met the front wall.

Arch noted the top hinge had rusted off, and the other two could use a good oiling. He shook his keys from his front pocket and sifted through them until he found one the color of dull gold. Two tries and the tumblers clicked. With a weary groan, the heavy front door squeaked and opened inward.

The distinctive aroma of mildew filled their nostrils, but the group conceded it wasn't as bad as they had anticipated. The sun filtered through the dirty, vine-encased windows, and a fuzzy haze of dust filled the room. Yet everything appeared to be perfectly in place.

"It's as if someone lived here, then just suddenly disappeared one day," Ro observed.

There was a plaid fabric sofa and wooden rocking chair in the living room. Dust covered the rough-finished hardwood floors, and an oval braided rug covering the majority of the room, adding a homey, lived-in atmosphere to the room. A few wooden shelves were set against the paneled walls. On either side were candle-filled wall sconces. There were a few books, an oil lantern, and a framed display of handmade fishing flies populating the shelves. A small table with two high back chairs sat under a window. On the table a chess set was displayed as if two people who were playing would be back to finish.

Nothing was out of place, but everything was completely swallowed with dust. Fiona gagged as Ezra fluffed the cushions of the couch, and dust billowed toward the ceiling.

Ro wandered into a small room that contained bunk beds on one wall and a folding cot that was propped against the other wall. In between was a small end table with a lamp and more books on a lower shelf. She noticed a few boxes under the bed but nothing else in that room. A shower curtain draped across the threshold served as a makeshift door to provide a modicum of privacy.

The living room opened to a combination kitchen/dining area with a small table and four chairs similar to the high-backed ones in the living room. Countertops lined two walls in a 90-degree angle. The far one was cut to hold a large deep sink. Inside the sink were two gray buckets.

"What are the buckets for," Indya asked.

"To carry water with, of course," Arch answered.

Indya stared from the buckets to the old wood stove with a kettle on top to the large stone fireplace held a cast iron cauldron hanging from a hook. "It's like something out of a history book. I can't believe I am seeing this," she whispered in mixed awe and revulsion.

"I can't believe we have to live this," Fiona added. She gazed about the kitchen with a puzzled look on her face. "Where's the refrigerator?" she asked.

This is a hunting cabin," Arch explained. There isn't a refrigerator."

"There's no refrigerator? What did you do to keep things cold?"

"Well, when we came out to hunt, we were usually only here for a few days," Arch answered. "We always brought a cooler with us. It kept the ice cold for as long as we needed it."

"I'm just grateful the cabin is still standing," Piper added. "I wasn't sure what to expect, but you know what? This is actually pretty great, all things considered. Arch, thank you for letting us come here with you."

A half-grin played across his face. "No problem. Of course.

But really, this is it guys. I did say it wouldn't be much. But I think it's pretty safe and definitely secluded. And let's face it—it beats the alternative."

"Oh man, I really like it." Leo was smiling. He was in his element in the woods, and the group could tell he was happy to not have to live in a tent again.

"Really?" Keno asked

"It's better than some places I slept."

"Where's the bathroom?" Zane asked. And he and Ronny looked around together.

Arch pointed to the right. "If I remember correctly it's about 25 yards that way."

"Outside?" Ronny was the one to speak up this time. "You mean, like an outhouse? A real, honest-to-goodness outhouse?"

"Yes."

"So... there's no running water? And if we need to go... we have to go..."

"What I mean is—this is a rustic cabin, not a hotel. Years ago there was electricity, but it's been off for a while. Nobody's paid a bill here in years. Which is a good thing. If we were hooked up to the electric grid, someone would definitely know we were here, right?"

"What about sinks for washing dishes and clothes, and bathing?"

"There's one in the kitchen," Ronny volunteered.

"Yeah, but no faucet. Just a drain. Remember that creek we crossed coming in?" Arch asked. "It's spring-fed. That's where our water comes from."

Fiona was starting to look distraught. "So we take a bath *out there*? Brush our teeth *out there*? And we'll have to wash clothes and dishes *out there*. Is that what you're suggesting?"

"No, I'm not *suggesting* anything," Arch answered.

"I think what he's saying is—that *is* where all that kind of activity will be done at. It's not a suggestion," Leo noted, then added, "Arch did say this place was off the grid."

Arch nodded in agreement. "Look, maybe we can figure out some kind of chamber pot system for when you need to...you know, go in the middle of the night. And eventually we might be able to figure out a way to pipe water from the spring into the house. But for now, we just gotta make the best of it."

He steered them outside. On the porch a swing hung limply by one chain. The other chain was snapped in half, and the broken part drug along the wood planks as the wind blew the swing in a lazy arc. Everyone stared sadly at it—an unspoken metaphor for the life before them, hanging by a fragile chain, driven by forces they couldn't see or control, liable to fall at any moment.

Ty finally broke the silence. "Let's unload the cars."

18

Keno's eyes grew wide. "Holy cow. They may have called us all crazy. But we're some real doomsday preppers here."

"Look at how much stuff we got!" Ty joined the group to admire the piles.

Leo shattered their high spirits as he added the last of the cases of drinking water to the stash laid out before them. "It won't last as long as you'd think," he said. "But it is a good start."

Keno elbowed Ty and grinned as if this was the greatest joke in the world. "This might all blow over by next week anyway, right?"

"Let's hope so, but I doubt it," Ronny interrupted. She couldn't help but think about all those people, innocent and unknowing, left out there—like her family. She took a deep breath and tried to put it out of her mind.

While unloading the cage of chicks, Piper also grabbed the brown bag that accompanied her purchase.

"What's in there?" Ro asked.

Piper reached in and pulled out a handful of envelopes. "Seeds. My Grandma used to garden and always said, *seeds are a lifeline we can't survive without.* So when I saw the display of them by the checkout at the Co-op, I grabbed everything that I could."

"Great thinking. And that's something we need to get to work on right away," Leo added. "Some of that stuff will take months to grow."

Fiona walked back to the porch with Piper. "Where's your Grandma now?" she asked.

"In a nursing home." Piper paused on the first step. Instead of continuing she swallowed hard as the realization set in—she might not see her grandmother in a very long time. Maybe not ever. "I was going to see her tomorrow. It's the weekend, and I go to see her almost every weekend."

Fiona could see the tears form before they fell and put her arm around Piper's shoulders to comfort her. "You'll see her soon. I know you will."

19

All supplies had been moved inside, inventory was being completed, and room was being designated for storage. Ty dusted off the rocking chair in the living room, then sat and surveyed his survival gear—his bow and arrows and the collection of fishing poles he hurriedly grabbed from his place. He usually kept his gear in order in a back corner of the closet, but in the haste to gather things as quickly as he could, everything became a jumbled mess. He was now pulling hooks from feathers and strings from mismatched reels. Silently he cursed his mistake.

Leo was outside inspecting his car. He drove a Ray, the newest solar prototype car on the market. It was the latest trend emerging in the auto world. And even though electric cars were relatively common, the Ray boasted the latest innovations in solar technology, and had claimed the sweet spot among the tree-hugger set.

Everyone thought it was pretentious when I bought this, he mused. *But now, it'll provide a solid source of power for lights and such. Particularly good for the baby chicks. But I have no idea how to connect the solar panel in the roof to anything outside the car.*

Zane had brought a gas-powered generator. Since gasoline

was a precious commodity, they all realized the generator could only be fired up for emergency situations. Still, it might serve until they could figure out the solar panel conundrum. For now Zane stood by Leo trying to figure out if there was a way to use the panel without completely dismantling the car.

"Wouldn't want to trash your high-dollar eco-mobile if this whole thing blows over next week," he joked.

"Oooh, you guys getting us electricity for the cabin?" Ro bounced down the stairs to the front lawn.

Ty followed behind her and caught Leo's eye. "Actually," he interjected, "the baby chicks are a higher priority than our personal comfort. We need them to thrive so they can provide a steady source of food. They need the electricity we can manage to produce just to keep them warm. Would you see if you can find a lightbulb that's still good in there?"

"Sure," she said, unsure of whether he was being serious or just messing with her mind. She decided to err on the side of caution and walked back inside.

"Hey guys, need any help?" Arch walked over to the car.

"To be honest, I have no idea what I'm doing here," Leo confessed.

Arch laughed. "Okay, let me take a look. Electronics is sort of my thing."

Arch spent the next few hours moving things around to get a better look at the vehicle's wiring system and computer interface. By the time the sun dropped to the horizon, Arch was smiling. He had a plan.

Over a dinner of canned chili and corn, both heated in their cans set in a fire outside in a makeshift fire pit, Arch explained how he might be able to make a simple conversion that would allow the car's solar panel to feed into the house's long dormant power box. The problem was getting the car close enough to make the tie-in work. The box was too surrounded by trees, and a number of tall oaks would need to be cleared away to make room. Until they could clear those trees, their only source of electricity would the the gas generator.

20

As the evening wore on, Leo emptied his backpack and pulled out an emergency radio. It was small and red with a small solar surface on the top and a winding mechanism on the side.

"Dude! That thing is cool." Ezra sat down across from him at the table. "Does it work?"

"Man, I hope so. I haven't used it in years, but I can't imagine it wouldn't." He turned it to the emergency station, flipped the switch on, and began winding. Within seconds a broken news report came from the small speakers on the front.

A deep male voice warned that anyone out on the street "would be shot or arrested. Martial Law is now in order." As Leo continued to wind the radio brief reports told of how the country was at war with itself. Phrases such as "People killing people to take what they can... Looting everywhere... Hoarding by many..." were spoken by anxious reporters. One woman, who sounded as if she was crying, said she was amazed at how quickly the chaos escalated.

A replay of an announcement by the president warned everyone to stay put. He went on to say that those needed transportation to Freedom Camps should board buses that would be making rounds starting in the morning. "Be ready with your family," he admonished. "Remember, only life-saving medications and medical equipment can be brought. Do not attempt to bring any other possessions. Food, water, and clothing will be supplied at the relocation facility."

Leo looked up and surveyed the stunned and sad expressions on the faces of his friends surrounding him. Fiona's wide eyes poured tears, and Ro dropped her face into her hands.

Keno's anger overflowed. "Oh yeah; sounds perfect. *Freedom* Camps. What a joke! *We'll take care of you*—until we're tired of taking care of you. Pathetic lies."

"You don't know that's what will happen," Zane suggested, although he was cautious with his words. "Maybe the government is just doing the best they can with a bad situation."

"Where would you rather be right now?" Arch asked, looking in Zane's direction.

"With my family," Ronny answered. She was also in tears.

"You didn't have to come," Keno said more harshly than he intended. "And no one's forcing you to stay. You want to go home to your family—go. Don't let the door hit you in the butt."

Zane gave a him a withering look, but Ronny diffused the situation by saying, "No; I didn't mean I wanted to be at home with my family. I meant I wish my family was here—with me. I just wish they were here. I don't want to go anywhere. We made the right decision."

The reports faded when Leo stopped winding. Silence filled the room until Ty finally broke it by saying what everyone else was thinking: "So much for this thing blowing over in a couple of days. Looks like were in it for the long haul."

21

It was a calm, mild night. Indya sat on the front porch dangling her legs over the side, and Ty leaned against the column to her right. Lightning bugs emerged drifting up from the ground. There were only a few now, but Indya knew that within a few months the night would be covered with them. A sliver of a moon sat low in the sky, but without light pollution to block their view, there were so many stars as far as an eye could see. A blanket of them covered the sky. Crickets and tree frogs sang, turning the silent night into nature's chorus.

"Ty, you should go on to bed," Indya breathed. "To be honest with you, I don't think I'm going to sleep much tonight. You can take the couch. I'll be fine with the floor."

If Ty heard her, he made no response. Instead he said, "I just can't believe this is happening. I mean, I can't wrap my head around it. Can you?"

Indya stared into the night in the direction of the creek. "I just wanna know what really *is* happening."

Ty answered with a deep sigh.

Indya changed the conversation. "Look at all this. How amazing! I never knew this much beauty existed in nature— not any of this, actually. The city lights swallow it all up. And the sounds—so comforting, yet almost alien. What makes those incredible sounds?

"Crickets. They sing. It's so relaxing, isn't it?" Ty asked.

"Seems louder than the buses and traffic in the city, yet not obtrusive like man-made noises. It's the kind of background noise you could actually sleep to."

"I don't know about that."

Indya looked in his direction in the darkness.

"How can you say it's relaxing? I'm a city boy. It sounds kinda creepy to me."

"No, it's calming," she whispered. "I never paid much attention to that before now I guess."

His voice hinted at an undefined sadness. "I'm going to bed. At least I'm going to try to get some sleep. I suspect we'll have a big day ahead of us tomorrow."

"Good night Ty. And we'll be fine. We all have each other. We came here together, and we'll get through this the same way."

He nodded. "I hope you're right. Guess time will tell."

22

It rained for three days. That third night after dinner the group sat in a circle in the living room. They ate cinnamon coffee cake as a rare dessert. It was a recipe that Piper's grandma passed down to her. The group was getting homesick, and together they reminisced about their families. Slowly pieces of each person's past were revealed.

Piper talked about her dad leaving her and her mom after she was born. He was in the army, and for his next assignment he told her mom that he was leaving—alone. She took care of Piper the best she could, but she became very sick.

"Stage four pancreatic cancer," Piper explained. "Before she passed away we moved in with my grandma. After mom passed, grandma did her best to raise me, but she was old. I know it was hard on her. Putting her in that nursing home was one of the hardest things I've ever had to do, but with her advanced age there was really no other choice. I couldn't give her the care she needed. And that's why I'm at the university working on my BSN degree—so I'll know that she's getting the level of medical attention she deserves. I had hoped that maybe I'd be able to move her back in with me once I had the necessary knowledge and qualifications to care for her myself. Doesn't look like that's going to happen now."

Ty opened up about his parent's divorce. "My dad lives across the country with his new family, and my mom is settled in with her new family in Florida. I'm kind of the odd man out, left in the middle trying to find some kind of direction amid the carnage. It's like, I'd rather not be around them, than to be in the same room with them and feel like I didn't belong there."

An awkward silence followed, but Indya broke it by telling about her life in the city. "I've never known any other kind of existence," she confessed. "I've never even driven a car, much less owned one. In the city, you could get anywhere you wanted to go on the metro, or by taking a ride-share. My folks raised me to be independent, and I loved being single and on the go all the time. Mom is—or was—a lawyer, and dad works on Wall Street... a mortgage banker or something like that. Even with their prestigious titles they always lived a moderate lifestyle. The cost of living is so high in that area, they never wanted to get trapped by what daddy always called Golden Handcuffs. It's been nearly a year since I went back home to see them. That might be what I regret the most at this moment. I wonder if I'll ever see them again?"

"I feel like I'm in an AA meeting," Leo quipped. "Hi, my name is Leo, and I'm a refugee from the total collapse of society."

A wry chuckle circulated among the friends, then Leo continued. "Seriously, I've never been comfortable talking about my family. I got into a bit of trouble over smoking pot when I was a kid. The second time my folks got into the whole *tough love* thing and sent me to counseling. Not that I completed that program. I just sorted of drifted through high school, crashed in a friend's garage for a while. I only went to college because student loans offered a bed and meals. I didn't really have a plan about what came after graduation." Now it was his turn to snort a laugh. "Guess I don't have to worry about paying back those student loans now."

Fiona raised her hand as if they were still in class. The progeny of a wealthy family, Fiona's father was Colombian and her mother was of Korean descent, giving her a striking, exotic appearance. The combination of beauty and wealth had been intimidating to most people only a week ago. Now, it didn't seem to matter at all.

"Unlike Indya's family that practiced frugality, my parents loved to flaunt their wealth. They thought it made them better than everyone else. My daddy used to tell me all the time, 'Fiona, you are worth more than most men will ever be able to give you,' and I believed him. I don't know, maybe at one time that was true, from a strictly materialistic viewpoint. I mean, my monthly allowance was more than—well, none of that matters now. The truth is, I used to feel superior. If I wanted something, I bought it. I didn't give it a second thought. Designer labels don't haul water though. I can't buy my way out of this situation." She hung her head, embarrassed at the realization. "Looking back over my life, I am ashamed. My family was obnoxious; the way the acted toward everyone, even their friends. Honestly, I don't want to be that way. I don't know if I'll ever see them again. I don't know if I'll ever see my boyfriend again, or if we are even still a couple. And... I'm afraid of being alone."

Ro put her arm around Fiona's shoulders and held her while she sobbed softly.

When it was his turn to talk, Ezra used the time to tell how he turned from religion in defiance of his conservative

Christian upbringing. "I resented being forced to go to church and to a private Christian school. I just wanted to know the truth, you know? I wanted to understand more of what life was all about. Honestly, with Mr. Harrison's class, I was just testing the waters. But now, with everything that's gone down, man, I'm even more confused than ever. I wish there was just a simple answer. But I'm guess there's not one."

Keno was openly weeping by the time the discussion got around to him. Memories of the past haunted him, and he confessed that he was a horrible person. "I can't get past that day on the field when I told Ty to "Get your white ass off the ground! We got a game to play." I was such a jerk!"

"It's all good," Ty said. "I forgave you a long time ago. All you got to do is forgive yourself."

Keno wipe the back of his hand across his eyes, nodded, and flashed a brief smile. "I'm just glad to call you my friend now. I'm a changed man, and I'm determined to live like it."

"I was the quintessential beauty queen growing up," Ro confessed. "At first I liked it. I mean, what girl doesn't love getting all dressed up and having people tell you how beautiful you are, and getting your picture taken. It can be exciting. But after a while, I just started feeling like I was being used; like I was a piece of meat in the marketplace. The competition got to be really unhealthy, and all the girls were just mean. What started out as fun turned into nothing but business. I wanted to quit and just have a normal life, but mom wouldn't hear of it. She said the only way I'd get to college was on pageant scholarships, and unless I wanted be a waitress for the rest of my life I needed to stop whining and win those pageants."

"Wow," Indya exclaimed. "That was harsh."

"I don't think she ever meant to hurt me," Ro said. "I think she was just scared I'd end up like her—a single mom, stuck in a deadend job with no future, no way out, and no hope. I just wish I could talk to her again."

"My first name is Gerald," Arch announced. "I was named after my dad. Gerald Archibald. Since he went by Gerry, they called me Archie. Yeah, I know, I got all the comic book ribbing while growing up. Middle school was the worst. Everybody wanting to know if I preferred Betty or Veronica. That got old real fast."

A lighthearted chuckle ripped through the room, and they encouraged him to continue.

"By the time I got to high school I had shortened it to just *Arch*. I loved computers and electronics." He barked a short laugh and added. "I used to take apart small appliances around the house to see how they worked. Most of the time I managed to put them back together the same way they came apart, but the microwave oven turned out to be a bit more complicated than my fifteen-year-old brain could comprehend. Let's just say, mom wasn't happy when she tried to defrost a roast. I won't say it went nuclear, but—"

The chuckles turned into true laughter and even a few belly laughs before settling to a comfortable silence.

Ronny reached for Zane's hand. "Zane and I have been dating since we were freshmen," she said. "There's nothing particularly exceptional about me. I'm not rich or beautiful or super smart. I guess I'm just your typical, middle-class girl-next-door. My mom was a stay-at-home mom and my dad was in management at a clothing manufacturing company. I have a younger brother, and we all lived in the suburbs of Trenton, New York."

She dropped her head into his hands. "We were a normal, happy family. I don't know how I'm going to do this without them. Every break I had from school I was at home."

Zane picked up where Ronny left off. "I'm pretty boring too. My family is normal. No real drama at home. I have an older brother and younger sister. She's at Penn State. I saw them at Christmas, some summers. Most of the time I stayed here or went with Ronny to her family's home."

The conversation waned. Nobody needed to say anything else. There was a general feeling of comradarie that came from knowing each other a bit better, and an air of appreciation for what each member of the group brought to the cabin. And equally important, there was a sense of loss for what had been left behind.

23

When the rainy weather broke and the sun finally emerged, life for the group moved to more outdoor, nature-related activities. Ronny sat in the adjoining field and used wildflowers to mindlessly make headbands. She was distracted and lay back, staring up at the blue sky. She wondered where her family was. Did they stay in their home? Where they forcibly shipped off to a Freedom Camp? If they managed to somehow escape, she had no idea where they would go. Deep in her heart she doubted they'd even try to leave. Deeper still, she wondered if they were even still alive. If not, then was there anyone from her former life was still alive?

Ro joined her and stretched out parallel to her on the grass. No one said a word for a while; each was lost in her own thoughts. Finally, Ronny broke the silence. "I don't even know what day of the week it is."

Ro was quick to supply the answer. "Based on the calendar we made, it's Wednesday the 5th." She plucked at long blades of grass at her side and added, "Not that it matters."

"Wednesday, huh? Is it? I feel like it's a Sunday; or maybe even a Monday. I never thought I'd need one of those cheesy calendars we used to get from the insurance company or bank. All I had to do was whip out my cell phone. But there are no cell phones or computers anymore. At least, none we can access. Funny how you miss the most insignificant things." She sat up and threw the headband she'd been weaving to the ground. It fell to pieces as it came to rest in the grass. "I used to call mom every Sunday afternoon. I haven't talked to her in so long, I feel like I'm gonna forget her voice."

Ro picked up the flower ring and gently rewove the stems. She laid it gently on Ronny's head, smoothed down some loose hairs, and smiled softly. "I guess we all miss family in our own ways. We just have to come to grips with the idea that now, we are each other's family. And if it's just for now, that's cool. But if it turns out to be longer; if it turns out to be forever, then so be it. We're what we have. If, God forbid, our families are gone—I hope they are in a better place. And I most certainly can't wait to join them in Heaven one day. But until that time, we need to be here for each other."

They sat beside each other in the field, talking and fashioning headbands for the rest of the girls, and watched the horizon as the sun sank lower in the west. While the sun hung above the horizon, they wandered to the edge of the woods and picked blackberries that were turning fat and luscious. They chatted about chores that needed to be assigned and work that needed to be done to make the cabin a more livable space. Their harvest complete, the two friends turned toward home.

"I have to admit something to you," Ro said before they reached the cabin's yard.

Ronny stopped and turned toward her as Ro continued. "There is someone here that I may have a slight crush on. I don't want to say anything, and I doubt he'd ever feel the same."

Immediately Ronny's thoughts turned to model-perfect Ty

with his short cropped curls and piercing blue eyes. "He's very good looking. I think Ty would like you too if you just talk—"

"It's not Ty," Ro said under her breath, clearly embarrassed. "I shouldn't have said anything."

"Oh, I'm sorry, Ronny countered. "I just thought he'd be the one. I mean, he's athletic, muscular, and not to mention one of the best looking guys on campus. Well of course, other than *my* man." They laughed.

Ro touched her arm shyly. "I'm actually not all that experienced with boys. I know that sounds crazy in this day and age. The truth is, I haven't really even dated too many guys. Dawson was my first real boyfriend—and let's face it, he wasn't much to write home about. But anyway..."

"Come on. Out with it," Ronny demanded. "The suspense is killing me."

"Alright. It's—it's Arch, okay?"

Ronny's eyes grew wide, and a muffled, "No way. You're kidding," escaped from her lips along with a single, incredulous laugh. She tried to picture the beauty queen next to her having a crush on the group's resident computer nerd, and the giggles could not be contained. Arch—the shy, reserved, hyper-intelligent, ham radio-listening, slightly overweight, computer master, quiet guy who would rather find a rock to crawl under than talk to a pretty girl. He was Ro's complete opposite.

"You have a crush on *Arch?*" Ronny immediately embraced Ro watching to not smash the berries she carried. "I think that is... amazing! Oh hon, I'll do everything in my power to keep your secret, but it's too good to hold back for long. Please, just let me be there when you tell him. I hafta see his face turn 20 shades of red."

Ro threw a berry at Ronny. "I knew I shouldn't have told you."

"Oh no. I'm glad you did. But I think it is more important that you tell him."

24

It was Leo's day to split fire wood. He decided the earlier in the morning he could do it, the better the chance of him not getting over-heated. Even though it was the middle of summer, wood was essential. They needed wood for the stove to cook with and to heat water for bathing and washing clothes and dishes. That fire never went out. Matches and starter fluid were too precious to waste by starting a new fire every day. And there was the stock of wood that would be needed to heat the cabin that needed to be cut and stacked. Better to have the supply laid in while the weather was still accommodating.

Keeping the fire going constantly had the unpleasant side effect of heating the inside of the cabin to an uncomfortable temperature, resulting in the group gathering on the porch to escape the growing heat in the house. Most cradled cups of coffee that they sipped slowly and appreciatively as they watched Leo swinging his axe. He was in a rhythm and barely noticed his friends observing his labors. Ty took the last swallow from his mug, laid it on the top step, and then bounded across the yard to Leo.

"Can't I give you a hand?" Ty said as he laid a piece of wood vertically on the stump.

Leo handed the axe to his friend and breathed out, "Thanks man. Everyone has a lot to do today, and it looks like it's gonna be a scorcher. I just don't wanna be caught out here around lunchtime. You think it's hot now? Whowee! It's gonna be miserable by then."

Ty looked back at the porch. The group appeared to have come to the same conclusion as Leo, and started moving toward their assigned chores. Ronny and Zane picked up baskets and headed toward the garden. Fiona collected the mugs and headed toward the wash basin in the kitchen. Piper hung back and leaned against the door frame, still sipping from her coffee and admiring the boys who had stripped off their shirts while they continued chopping wood.

Fiona returned from the kitchen with a broom and dust-pan, and held them out toward her friend. She caught her eye and grinned. "Are you supervising, or did something else catch your eye?"

"A little of both," Piper laughed and traded the broom for her mug.

~

Arch proved to be the star fisherman of the group. It seemed he could practically talk the fish into the net, so it was natural that he was assigned the task of providing the group with fresh fish. No one was surprise when he came home with a stringer full of trout or sunfish. That evening was no different. Dinner consisted of the fresh catch of the day, rice, and the special treat of the first tomatoes from the garden.

"Two things money just can't by, Ronny quipped. "Love... and a home grown tomato."

As Ronny and Keno prepared dinner in the kitchen Ezra tried to teach Zane the finer points of playing chess. When they had first arrived, Ezra was the only one that knew the game. Now, he had managed to lose to both Arch and Leo. Ezra didn't seem to mind. He played for the love of the game and was just happy to have others to share it with.

Leo was busy washing up after having chopped and stacked two ricks worth of wood. There was still some left to stack as the sun hung low on the horizon. He figured they could finish it in the morning.

Across the room Piper studied Leo. He wiped his face dry after standing back up from rinsing off. His brown curls glistened, as did his green eyes by the candle light.

He was very handsome. The thought formed unbidden in Piper's mind. He had always sported a close trimmed beard, but today it looked longer, fuller... softer. She wanted to reach out and touch it to see if it was.

Leo suddenly had the odd sensation that someone was watching him. He glanced in her direction, and Piper quickly looked back down at the book she appeared to be trying to read. Her cheeks grew warm, and she wondered if he saw her staring. When she dared to look up again, Leo was smiling crookedly at her.

He had.

25

A blood curdling scream echoed through the cabin followed by cries for help from Keno. Ronny and Piper rushed
onto the porch and saw Indya laying on the ground clenching
her hand. Keno cradled her in his arms.

"She was helping me with the wood chopping," he
explained through broken breaths. "I chopped, she moved
the split pieces. She didn't get her hand back quickly enough.
I tried to pull up, but I caught the outside of her hand."

Blood was pooling and falling between her fingers as she
gripped the injury tightly. Ronny rushed into the kitchen
to grab the first aid kit while Piper took charge of Indya.
Together they fumbled through the contents of the first aid
kit and extracted a roll of gauze, an alcohol pad, a packet of
antibiotic cream, and some butterfly bandages.

"I don't know if this will be enough, but it's all we've got."
Ronny said.

Piper nodded, and the girls set to work cleaning Indya's
cut the best they could.

Piper pulled Ty aside and said, "She's going to need stitches.
I don't believe we even thought to get a sewing kit."

"Okay. I'll see what we can find," Ty whispered. He turned
to Arch's side. "Is there any kind of sewing kit in the cabin? I

didn't see one when we did inventory of the stuff we brought. I can't believe we didn't think of that as an essential item. Too late now."

"I don't think so. We've been through the whole place when we settled in, and didn't see one, so..."

"Is there any place close by that we might be able to find one?" Ty interrupted. "A neighbor, a convenience store?"

"The closest neighbor is a dairy farm a few miles up the road that way." He pointed toward a hillside in the distance. A faint fenceline was visible in the distance, but no one in the group recalled seeing or hearing any cows since they arrived.

"Well, we wanted to explore the area," Ty said. "Guess there is no time like the present."

"I'm coming with you," Keno said. "I need to do something to help. I'm so, so sorry!"

"I'm coming too," Piper spoke up. "I have a better idea of what will work from a nursing perspective. Hope the neighbors are friendly—but let's take a gun or two, just in case."

Footsteps coming up the gravel driveway alerted the group that someone was approaching. Indya, who had been lying on her back on the porch with her arm straight up in the air, was the first to recognized the trio of friends returning. She moved to a sitting position and shot a questioning look at the three as they quickstepped toward to her.

"Well?" she asked.

Smiles crossed their faces as Keno raised a sewing kit above his head in a victory salute.

"You found one!" she beamed.

"We did," Piper affirmed. "Even scored tooth numbing

cream. In a pinch it'll do as a local anesthetic. Might help to ease the pain of the needle when I put in the stitches. Speaking of which, sooner is better than later. Let me wash my hands and get everything ready, and I'll get you stitched up."

"Thank you." Indya had tears in her eyes. "And I'm so thankful to God that we have a nurse among us."

Piper smiled. "Not a nurse yet, but hopefully I've got enough of the basics to help get us by. As long as nobody needs major surgery or a baby delivered, we should be fine."

Everyone gathered around the patient and pseudo nurse as Ty recounted their adventure. "We found the dairy farm a couple of miles up the road, just where Arch said it would be. We didn't see another soul on the road. It was nerve-wracking to knock on their door. I mean, we didn't know what to expect, and truth be told I was preparing for the worst. Instead this old lady answers the door with a smile on her face. She just looked happy to have company, and invited us in. Then an old guy shuffles in from the dining room and offers us coffee."

"Jack and Claudia Blount," Piper chimed in. "They were probably in their late seventies, maybe their eighties. And they were so sweet! Claudia offered me her sewing kit."

"I told them that we would be glad to trade for the kit," Keno interrupted, "but Claudia would have none of it. She just said, 'Take it, and be blessed.' I didn't know that sort of kindness was left in the world."

Ty resumed the story. "When we left, I told them that if they needed something to send a shot into the air, and we'd come a'running to try to help them. You know what Mr. Blount said?"

Everyone except Indya and Piper shook their heads.

Indya was wincing to control the pain, and Piper fought for concentration.

Ty continued, "He said he had never liked guns and didn't own one. But that was—before. Now that it is impossible to buy one, he wishes he had one."

"You know, a dairy cow might be a nice trade for one of our shotguns," Ezra suggested. "We actually have more than we need."

"My thoughts exactly my friend," Ty winked.

26

"What are you doing up so early?" Ezra ask Leo as he rolled over from his place on the floor.

"I couldn't sleep. And just as I suspected…" He trailed off.

By now Ezra was up and walking toward him. The sun was just starting to rise, and dark shadows still covered the floor of the cabin. "What did you suspect?"

"We are down to the last few cases of water. Did anyone think to get any water filters or bleach?"

Ezra took in a deep breath before yawning it out. "I don't know. I thought I saw some bottles of bleach in the original supply stash, but I could be mistaken."

"I don't remember. The only jugs I thought we had were cooking oil."

"Maybe that was it. I don't know man. It's too early for this."

"Well we gotta figure something out. I mean, we can drink creek water if we have to, but who knows what kind of contamination is in that water? Parasites and bacteria from critters pooping in it, or dying and rotting in it upstream. And what if the creek goes dry?"

"Okay, okay. I get it. Running out of drinking water—bad. Clean drinking water—good. We'll have a group meeting, maybe suggest we keep the bottled water for emergency only.

For the time being we can boil water to disinfect it, and refill some of the empty bottles."

"Good idea." Leo agreed.

"And if there is bleach, we can use that too."

As soon as the group as a whole stirred, Leo called a meeting and explained the water situation. Everyone agreed to the need for conservation, so Leo, along with Zane and Ronny, volunteered to be first on water duty. After a quick breakfast the trio grabbed buckets and headed to the creek.

Leo pointed to the left. "We need to be further up that direction when we fill the buckets."

"Why?" Zane asked. "What's up there?"

"We need to be upstream, past the point of where we've bathed and washed dishes," Leo explained. "We need to find a nice, free-flowing area, preferably where some moss or other natural filters remove most of the contaminants."

"Makes sense," Ronny said. "Maybe we should rethink where we bath and wash clothes."

Leo nodded in agreement. "First things first. Right now we need to find the best source for drinking water."

Zane pointed at a potential site where the creek flowed peacefully over a bed of pea sized gravel.

"I don't see why we'd even need to boil this water," he said. "It looks and smells better than anything that ever came out of the faucet at my old home." Zane held a cupped handful of cold water to his nose then continued. "I've always heard if the water is running it's fine to drink; that its the stagnant water that just sits in pools that breeds parasites."

Ronny squatted beside him and dipped some in her hand to inspect as well. "I still don't know if I trust it. But I do think standing water would be worse."

"Well, this water is running freely. I think it should be okay," Zane noted.

Ronny dumped the water she was holding back into the creek. "It looks good and smells good, but where did it come from? We don't know what's upstream. There may not be any parasites, but what if there is some kind of fertilizer run-off from a farm or other kinds of pesticides or chemicals that might have gotten into the water since all this began?"

Zane shrugged. "Faint hearts never won fair maidens," he quipped. "I'm gonna try it. I'm thirsty, and I'm taking a drink." He dipped his hand into the creek, pulled it to his mouth and slurped up several large mouthfuls. "Mmm, sweet!" he declared.

"Famous last words," Leo said, coming up behind him. "I hope you don't regret that."

That evening terrible stomach cramps haunted Zane. Whether it was the water he drank or the squirrel that was battered with flour and fried in Crisco—Zane couldn't be sure. But one of them put him in bed early that night—and kept him running to the outhouse all night.

"Dude. We're supposed to go check traps tomorrow." Keno flopped down on the bunk above him.

"I'll be fine," Zane muttered with eye lids pressed shut. His stomach let out an unappealing rumble, and he groaned as he started yet another trek to the outhouse.

"Next time maybe you'll listen to your girlfriend," Ronny said with a sweet smile on her face.

Zane didn't look back. He just nodded and kept running.

27

The face Fiona made explained it all. She was utterly disgusted. Zane held the slaughtered rabbit by its hind legs at arm's length. Blood dripped from its neck.

"Dinner is served."

He walked past Fiona—who now covered her mouth with both hands—and continued. "And Ezra is bringing two smaller ones too. He's right behind me."

"What's wrong?" Ty asked her.

Pointing at his hands, she stressed, "*That* is what is wrong with me. It's gross. You want us to eat rabbit?"

"Rabbit, squirrel, chicken. Yeah, it's food. I thought you got over that whole vegan thing when the world came to an end," Ro said.

"I know, I know," she said. "I get it. Survival of the fittest and all that sort of thing. I just thought the extent of that would be me having to get over the fact that I may need to eat Bambi one day. I can handle a deer. Kind of. But, I mean, yesterday it was squirrel. And now—I don't know. A rabbit? I mean it's like eating Thumper!"

Zane chuckled. "Wait until I bag that big groundhog out back in the field."

Fiona gasped.

Keno laughed at her reaction, "Or that family of 'possums that roam around at night."

Fiona ran out past the field-dressed rabbit, holding one hand over her mouth and waving the other in the air. She encountered Ezra as she reached the last step. He held two more small rabbits, already skinned and gutted. "Do you think you guys could help me ease into this life, a little more gently, huh?" She leaned over and tried not to wretch.

Ronny walked out of the screen door, wiping her hands with a dish cloth. "Fiona, why don't you come help me make a batch of drop biscuits? Maybe it will get your mind off the meat. I'll cook the rabbits. Next time you see it will be when it's with some rice on a plate."

The guys tried hard to not laughed, but Fiona simply shook her head and followed Ronny back inside.

In the kitchen Ronny quickly gathered supplies and ingredients for the biscuits. They poured the bag of flour into a tall rectangle metal box to keep bugs out once opened. From there Ronny scooped out a few cups into one of the few mixing bowls they had. She added one scoop of powdered egg. "A real egg would be better. Two eggs would be perfect," she signed, "but until the chickens start laying, we have to make do. It's better than none."

To the flour she added a spoon of powdered milk, a pinch of baking powder, and generous amount of boiled water.

"Can you hand me the pan over there?" She directed with her head to a small metal baking sheet on the table.

Fiona did and backed away.

"Don't leave yet," Ronny said, mixing the bowl with a wooden spoon. "Grab that shortening there and coat the pan before I spoon these on it."

"Coat it? With what?" Fiona asked.

Ronny looked up. "Your hands."

Fiona looked at her in confusion and then to her hands but didn't say anything.

Ronny added, "Don't worry I trust your hands are clean. You haven't been doing anything to make them that dirty. Any bacteria that survives your handwashing will be killed when we bake these in the oven."

Fiona obediently scooped a dollop of shortening out of the container and wiped it on the surface of the pan. It was clear that cooking was a foreign activity for her.

Ronny ignored her discomfort and continued, "If it makes you feel better, everything you've eaten so far had someone's germs on it. And we're all still alive. Speaking of, when do you want to do kitchen duty?"

Fiona finished coating the pan, then used the same cloth Ronny wiped her hands on to remove the grease from hers. "I don't know if I'll ever be able to do this."

"Sure you can. I have a feeling you'll get used to this life, my friend. After all, what choice do we have?"

28

Eventually everyone in the group settled into a comfortable routine. Each performed the chores they were best suited for, and the less pleasant labors were assigned by a *drawing from the hat* system. The result was every group member got to do tasks they enjoyed and were good at, and everyone shared in the tasks that no one really wanted to do. Trading chores was allowed, but not required. They took turns on the standard tasks of cooking, hunting, fishing, cleaning, chopping wood, and gardening, and they established a system for taking days off for socializing, relaxation, private devotional time, or for just doing nothing.

They quickly exhausted the limited supply of books in the cabin. No one had thought to bring additional reading material. In the recent past, they would simply download the latest novel to their Kindle or iPad. Now books were a luxury. Piper had even finished a Reader's Digest compilation of mysteries; something she would never have picked up in her previous life, but discovered it was a genre she thoroughly enjoyed and was happy to have available to read.

Without the normal level of chores to perform, Arch concentrated on tying flies based on the ones his grandpa had on display. Ronny snapped beans from the garden into a bowl, and Indya used the now indispensible sewing kit to repair lose buttons on one of Leo's shirts.

A comfortable silence reigned, and for a long while no one felt the need to break it. At last Ezra looked at Keno and said one solitary word. "Ready?"

Indya looked up. "Ready? Ready for what? Where are you guys going? I thought this was a day off."

Keno slipped on his boots. "It is, but that doesn't mean I want to just sit around all day. It's a beautiful day, and I want to go do something outside before it gets too hot."

"We're going on a supply run," Ezra explained. "And were going to take some time to scope out the neighborhood. So far the only people we've seen since we arrived at the cabin are Jack and Claudia Blount from the dairy farm. But there were a few other homes that we could see farther down the road. I think it's a good idea to get the lay of the land."

"Just remember our rule," Ro said from the far end of the couch.

Ezra recited it as if in class. "Rule Number One—and only rule we have so far—Thou Shalt Not Steal. Got it. We vow to only enter abandoned homes and to only search through abandoned cars. We'll scout things first just to make sure. The last thing we want is to alert the government of our existence, and we sure don't want to make any enemies of folks who might be just trying to survive... like us. If we see evidence of people coming or going, we move on. But if it looks like people have been relocated, or just left on their own before this all came down, it's game on."

"Just because nobody's home doesn't mean nobody lives there. What if their just gone for a while? Rule Number One: no stealing, remember?"

"Okay, okay. No stealing, Keno said. If a place appears to be abandoned and it doesn't look like anyone's coming back, maybe we can just, you know, *borrow* some stuff that we need—like tools, bedding supplies, and clothing. Anyone have any special requests that we should be on the lookout for?"

"Canned food. Cleaning supplies. Medications. Oh, and matches," Indya ticked items off on her fingers.

"I'd love something new to read," Piper added.

"We could use some gasoline for the generator," Arch mentioned." I know that gets pretty heavy to carry, but maybe if you find some, you can create a cache and we can come back for it."

"Feminine hygiene products," Ronny said from the table where she was playing a game of solitaire. "Napkins, tampons—at this point I don't think any of us are particularly picky."

Keno stuck his fingers in his ears and chanted, "La la la la la la la."

A blush crept up Ezra's neck and settled on his cheeks. "Oh man. I'll see what I can do, but I didn't expect to have to do that until I was married."

29

It had been five days since Ezra and Keno had made their initial reconnaisance of the area. With the exception of the Blounts, all of the homes they encountered were empty. It was as if the people had left for work one day and just never returned. Rather than breaking in to what might be someone's home, they had set thread traps on the doors. It was time to check the houses, and several of the group joined in on the expedition. If the threads were broken, they would know someone had been there—although they would not be able to tell if that someone was the owner, or an intruder.

The first home they returned to was small; one bedroom, no more than 700 square feet in size. It was quiet. The thread was undisturbed on the door, but the stillness made the situation unnerving. The yard was overgrown, although the sidewalk was still visible among the weeds. There were no cars in the driveway, but there were two full gas cans sitting by a push mower in a small outbuilding. Leo grabbed each can and set them by the back steps.

Ezra whipped out his pocketknife, jimmied the lock on the back door, and pushed it open. The place looked to have been abandoned long before the event happened. Thick dust blanketed empty counter tops, and the shelves were mostly bare. He stepped inside and looked for anything that might be salvageable. The only items usable were a plastic water pitcher, two light bulbs, and a small bag of cleaning cloths.

A lone twin-size mattress was balanced against the wall, and there was a threadbare love seat in the living room. Before they left, Indya pulled the curtains and rods down from the windows. She collapsed the rods into a two-foot section and rolled them along with the curtains together and stuffed both vertically into her backpack. "Never know," she said.

The guys said nothing. Ezra carved a signature checkmark into the doorframe to mark that they had already been there, while Leo picked up the fuel cans, and they all headed to the next house.

Nearly a mile of steady walking brought them to the second house on their list. It was easily twice the size of the first house. The back yard was fenced, but oddly did not have a gate to enter through. They checked the front door and found the thread trap still intact. The only entrance was the back door, which was inside the gateless fence. Leo and Ezra shared a masculine glance then leapt the chain link fence in one swift motion and trotted toward the back door.

Indya shook her head and sighed. "Men," she said, but she smiled all the same, then made her way to the front door. From the inside she could hear Leo shout, "All clear."

Then they all heard it—a small bark coming from inside the house.

A dog? Indya thought. *Ezra and Keno were here five days ago. They didn't say anything about hearing a dog. Poor thing must be scared. And starving.*

She twisted the front doorknob, but no avail. *Locked,* she fumed. She banged on the door and called out, "Hey guys, did you hear that? There's a dog in there. Be careful. It's probably scared and you can't be to careful around an animal that is scared."

Leo unlocked the door from the inside and pulled it open. the stench hit Indya like a tsunami of smell. It was obvious the dog had not been able to go outside to do it's business.

Ezra and Leo both had their noses hidden inside their shirts, and Indya started opening windows to help alleviate the smell. A quick survey revealed trashcans tumbled over and the contents scattered across the floor. Bags of bread and boxes of cereal had been pulled from the pantry and tore apart.

"Smart dog, fending for itself like that," Leo said. "I wonder where it is?"

"Here," Indya said softly. "Don't make any sudden moves. Poor thing looks to be terrified."

In the corner of the living room, wedged between a wall and the couch, a small dog stared at them from its hiding place. It appeared to be a terrier; its hair, probably once trimmed and beautifully groomed, was now shaggy and matted. Although obviously scared and likely dehydrated, the small creature did not appear to be viscous. After some encouragement, it shyly approached Indya.

Indya reached into her backpack and pulled out a bottle of water. She pour a small amount into her hand and offered it to the dog, who lapped it greedily and whimpered for more.

"Can one of you guys find me some kind of bowl," she asked, not taking her eyes from the dog.

Leo nodded and searched in the kitchen for a moment, then returned with a shallow dish. Indya placed it on the floor and poured in more water. She continued refilling the dish until the pup had drank its fill. Satiated at last, the little dog approached Indya, climbed into her lap, and pressed against her, shivering—whether in fear or relief, she couldn't say. Indya petted the pup and snuggled it close.

"Looks like you've found a new friend," Leo said.

"She's coming with us," Indya declared. Nobody argued.

"She?" Ezra inquired.

"Of course, *she*," Indya laughed. "And she and I are going to be good friends."

The guys set to gathering anything of use that would fit into their backpacks. There was a decent supply of canned goods in the pantry, some toiletries, even some feminine products.

"We can go back as the conquering heros now," Leo quipped, displaying the feminine napkins.

Indya just shook her head and spoke to the dog. "Men," she said.

The items from the Dog House, as Ezra dubbed it, along with the take from the first house filled their backpacks. They decide it was time to return to the cabin while there was still plenty of light.

On the long walk back they pondered how the dog managed to survive with no human to provide for her.

"Probably drank from the toilet until it ran dry," Leo ventured.

"And she did a number on the pantry," Ezra added. "Still, it's a miracle she survived."

When they told the story to the group that evening, everyone agreed the dog's name would be Miracle Mary. Or just Mary, for short.

"Sounds good to me," Indya said hugging the newest member of their family before passing her off to the next pair of arms waiting to love on her.

Piper held her close. "We could use something like her around here."

For a long moment the whole group was silent, as the same realization settled on them all. How many pets had been lost; their owners never returned. It was heartbreaking to think about.

30

"I think we use one of the houses we last visited as a midpoint as we expand our scouting area," Ezra suggested as everyone gathered in the living room for a group meeting.

"I vote for the one that wasn't the dogs bathroom," Leo automatically noted.

Indya nodded adamantly.

"Wait, what do you mean, *midpoint?*" Zane asked.

Ezra went on to explain, "We will eventually need to expand our search and scouting area. I think if we use the houses we clear as stopping points we'd be able reach further distances. I know in some cases we'd need to overpack supplies just to get us there, but we might come back with so much more. And who knows what all we might find out there."

"And remember, we haven't even gone that way yet." Ro pointed toward toward the northwest.

"True," Arch agreed. "Maybe we should try that way next. Then work our way out, like you suggested Ez."

"Okay. Then tomorrow let's plan to explore northwest. We'll see if there are any inhabited homes, and set some traps on any empty dwellings we find. Who wants to go this time?" Ezra asked.

"I'd like to go," Arch said.

"Me too," Ronny spoke out and then elbowed Zane. He lifted a finger. "And I'll lead them."

Arch laugh and then saluted him.

"Aye, aye captain. Lead us to battle."

Zane gave him a crossways glance, but Ronny burst out laughing. "I was thinking the same thing."

31

Keno leaned against the fence along the side yard. Beside him Arch whittled a stick into a sharp point, touching it every so often to ensure good progress was being made on his handiwork.

"What are you looking at?" Arch asked.

"You know, we've only followed the roads. We need try other directions too. Like, what's on the other side of those woods back there?" Keno motioned with his head.

"I really don't know." Arch shrugged. "I don't ever remember going far enough into them to get lost. The underbrush is pretty thick. It would take a lot of work to cut a path. But I think if you did you'd end up somewhere around Stone Hill Road."

The name of the road didn't mean much to Keno, but he knew that meant there might be more supplies that direction. I'm on garden duty now," he said. "But after lunch, I think I'll try to find a way through there. I'm curious what's on the road."

"Well, if you went out here and took a right past the first house you found I think Stone Hill is about two—no, probably three, more miles past that." Arch drew a crude map in the dirt at their feet.

Keno knew the first house was over a mile away. That would make a four mile trek just to reach Stone Hill. "How far would you say it would be through those trees?"

Arch stopped and thought a second before answering. "Maybe a mile. Maybe less than that I guess. Like I said though I never made it more than a few yards into the wood when we played in there as kids. But you gotta remember, I was pretty young. What seems like a long way might have only been a few steps. The perspective of youth, you know?"

Keno picked up the basket and headed toward the garden. As Arch turned to watch him, he saw Ro walking his way. She shyly smiled and took the spot Keno had vacated.

"How are you?" she asked.

He smiled back, his cheeks growing red. "Good. I thought I'd try my hand at gigging frogs." He showed her the pointed stick.

"Really?" Her eyes grew large.

"No." Arch laughed nervously, feeling suddenly awkward. "I'm actually making stakes for the tomato plants."

As if not hearing him she quickly continued. "I was just wondering what are you doing?"

He held up the stake, reminding her.

"No," she stopped him. "I didn't mean, literally what you're doing. I meant..." Now it was her turn to experience an awkward pause. She blew out a shy breath. "I mean... I wanted to see if you might want to go for a walk or something. With me."

A mix of surprise, shock, and delight played across Arch's face, and he fought a losing battle to keep the red blush from climbing up his neck to his cheeks. He nodded and allowed her to take his hand and lead him her toward the creek. Once they reached the bridge, she stopped and turned to face him.

Confusion mixed with concern was evident on Arch's face. "Is there something wrong?"

Ro didn't answer immediately. Instead she stood still, looking down, as if trying to find the right words to say. When at last she looked back up into his eyes, she simply shook her head, stepped forward, and in one smooth movement put her hands on each side of his face, pulled him toward her, and brushed his lips with a slow, sweet kiss.

The shock caused Arch to stumble backward into the railing, and almost fall into the creek. "Wha—what was—why did you…?

Instead of answering, Ro stepped forward and pulled him away from the edge of the bridge. This time she held him tight against her and kissed him more intently. This time Arch didn't pull away, but leaned into her, wrapped his arms around her, and pulled her into him. They allowed the kiss to linger, and after a full minute, Ro pulled away.

"I like you Arch. I just couldn't figure out a way to tell you."

"I—like you too." He smiled, leaned in and kissed her forehead lightly. "I just never thought a guy like me had a chance with girl like you, and…"

Ro cut him off with another kiss.

32

As Keno explored the path he created in the woods with Ty and Indya, Ezra chopped at the felled tree that once impeded the solar panel from the car. Fiona sat on the porch steps and washed dishes in a bucket between her legs. Arch and Ro cuddled on the swing snapping beans into a pot. Ronny and Zane laid in the shade, legs and arms wrapped around each other, resting from weeding in the garden. At the edge of the creek Leo sat close to Piper as they handwashed clothes. Beside them, Mary splashed around in the water, growling every so often as the water sprayed her in the face.

Fiona dried the last of the bowls and looked around, "Geez…You know, I don't think I can handle all this lovey-dovey crap that's going on around here."

Ro looked at Arch, beaming. He put his arm around her and pulled her close. It had been two weeks since the day she confessed her feelings. With each day they grew closer.

Leo and Piper on the other hand were taking the slow path, mostly denying the inevitable. Their trips together to fish or wash clothes didn't go unnoticed by the others. They knew eventually the truth would come out. For now it was fun to watch.

Fiona set the bucket with now clean dishes onto the porch,

and Ezra came to join her on the steps. She handed him the cup she'd been drinking from. He downed the rest of the water and thanked her.

"Ez, do you think we'll ever get back to normal again."

"Maybe." He fell back onto the porch, leaned on his right elbow, and wiped his brow with the neck of his shirt.

She looked up at the happy couple in the swing. "I don't mind it."

Ezra waited silently for her to continue and she thought a second before she did. "The normal. If this is the new normal I kinda don't mind it."

"What about your family? You have to miss them."

"Of course I do. I'm sure I always will. It's just that—I just know that if this is my new normal, I am happy I have all of you as a part of it."

"I don't get all religious very often, and I've never been big on destiny, but this— this doesn't feel like a coincidence. Us being all together. I mean, I have to believe we all ended up in that class at the same time for a reason." Ezra sat up.

"I agree," Arch said from the porch swing. "I'm proud to call you all my friends. I don't know if it was luck or fate, but I'm glad to have met Mr. Harrison who introduced me to my new family."

Epilogue

J oey Harrison was doing quite well. He and his family were living about 20 miles from where his class was staying in the cabin. He held the paper Arch had left on the pole and read the address again. He knew that lake region well.

Violence and economic depression were still the order of the day, with Martial Law still in place. Harrison's desire to visit his former students was tempered by prudence. It was not yet safe to leave his place for more than a few miles. Hopefully, as the country settled into it's new normal, and the flames of fury died down, hope would return.

As he sat with his young family on the front porch on his own cabin, he smiled. *Yes,* he thought, *those young people had listened. They had understood. They recognized the signs of the times, and were prepared.*

Because of that, they endured while so many others perished.

About the Author

KL Palmer calls herself *the working mother's author.*

Even though she hasn't (yet) written a book on how to be a better mom, or how to incorporate your personal life into your long work day; she did follow her dream and write a novel—or five. She hopes to inspire other working moms to write, or follow their dreams wherever they lead, and not give up.

One thing that sets her apart from others is her propensity to write what she calls *break chapters*—chapters short enough to take a bathroom break, commercial break, or smoke break away from life, with each averaging just two to three pages. She wants to bring reading back into the lives of busy people; to show that you can, in fact, enjoy a book and take time for yourself; and do so with the limited and precious spare time you have.

Born and raised in a quiet Amish-surrounded community in Pennsylvania, she now resides in Tennessee with her family. In addition to being employed full time in a corporate real estate position, Palmer remains passionate about her church and her writing. She jokes that her mind never shuts off. Even in the most inopportune time she's jotting down ideas for the next manuscript.

Just don't tell her boss!

Also By
KL Palmer

Pipe Dream

Aslo Available from
WordCrafts Press

The Mirror Lies
by Sandy Brownlee

House of Madness
by Sara Harris

Ill Gotten Gain
by Ralph E. Jarrells

Obedience
by Michael Potts

www.wordcrafts.net

Made in the USA
Columbia, SC
10 June 2021